PILLOW

MUSEUM

THE

PILLOW

MUSEUM

Stories

CLAIRE BATEMAN

FC2

TUSCALOOSA

Book Design: Publications Unit, Department of English, Illinois State University; Director: Steve Halle, Production Assistant: Jalissa Jones
Cover image: Six Studies of Pillows, Albrecht Dürer, 1493; Metropolitan Museum of Art
Cover design: Matthew Revert
Typeface: Adobe Jenson Pro

Library of Congress Cataloging-in-Publication Data is available from the Library of Congress.
ISBN: 978-1-57366-206-2
E-ISBN: 978-1-57366-908-5

Contents

Home Art   1
The Fleet Ones   3
A Day's Work   5
Tune-Up   9
Stretchies   12
Genius Status   15
Reversals   21
The House Sitter   23
Donations   32
Relics   34
The Pillow Museum   37
The Blue Telephone   41
Dear Oracle   45
The Underlife   50
Crossings   73
Ledger   75
Elemental   77
Pockets   81
Shore Patrol   85
Gravity Pajamas   86
Handiwork   88

Collectibles	90
Dig	94
Cake-Heart	96
The Quest	101
Going Under	102
The Last Space-Bearer	105
Universal Cognitive Maintenance	110
Reverse Paper	113
Literary Contrivances of the Future	115
Gloves	117
Recurrence	118
Monograph on a Giant Lullaby	119
Forests	123
The Day We Awoke to Find All the Animals Gone	125
The Bees	127
Teleology	128
Distance at Very Close Range	130
The Remedy for Haunting	134
Devices	136
Keepers	159
The Self-Correcting Language	161
The Sky Is Lifting	163
Hatchling	166
Product Details	167
Hurt	169
Bread	171
Tribe	173
Anomalous Teeth	174
Immersion Candles	176
The New Self-Soothing	177

The End of Shopping   179
Telling   182
Epochal   185
Fathoming   186
One Sleep   188

Acknowledgments   191

Home Art

It was snowing the night they had the fight about the glass piano whose music provided all the light in the house. She'd been playing while he went through the newspaper page by page.

"I'm tired," she told him. "I want to stop."

"I'm not done with the puzzles," he said.

She performed a disfigured rendition of Leonard Cohen's "Hallelujah" with obnoxious ornamentations, but he ignored her.

She said, "I need to set the dishes to soak before everything gets crusted over, so go ahead and take your turn." Actually, though, she planned to slip out through the kitchen door to feel the flakes swarming around her face. This kind of weather was increasingly rare—what a tragedy it would be to miss the very last snow in the world just so he could work the sudoku!

"It's my birthday for two more hours," he said, "so I'm still automatically exempt."

She plunked out the "Happy Birthday to You" song at quadruple speed in a sarcastic frenzy, then transitioned into a long run of Philip Glass backward, forward, upside-down, and fortissimo. She did a rageful Glenn Gould imitation, squeezing each note out ostentatiously through her sinuses. He didn't flinch.

By now, all that mattered was for domestic visibility to be *his* labor, so she brought down a crashing final chord, then stopped. Everything went dark.

"Play!" he shouted. She sat on her hands.

He stumbled over to the piano and felt around roughly until he found her wrists, yanked her hands out from under her, forced her fingers to the keys, and banged them up and down.

The light came up even brighter as she smiled in her victory.

The Fleet Ones

It's a fine time to be born with feet all over your body, though it does increase parental workload with so many little socks to wash, dry, and sort.

The multipedal move through the world in a combination of cartwheels, leaps, hops, and crisscross circumnavigations; it's speculated that because of their momentum, time slows down for them, so they experience more actual life. Some people even claim they move as fast as money itself, but that's impossible, of course, since nothing human can approach that velocity.

My sisters would never let me play with them when we were little because I couldn't keep up. Now they scuttle along the sides of buildings as they deliver packages through the windows, and leap from station to station, track to track in the subway.

Mother used to hold me on her lap and gently stroke my two little feet, reassuring me that I was special in my own way, but still I'd cry and ask why I had to be born so limited.

"The Holy Trinity of Amazon, FedEx, and UPS"—and here she'd half-close her eyes as she moved her fingers through the air with the sign of the sacred dollar—"uses algorithms for the number of runners to genetically engineer; we mustn't question their ways. And look, just like you, I've got only two feet, yet you can see that I have a lovely, happy life." But she'd been born before the enhancements, so that didn't count. I never mentioned this since I knew she was just trying to make me feel better.

Each night in my dreams I commit the federal-ecclesiastic crime of taking the family hand ax that hangs from a peg on the garage wall and cleaving off my sisters' feet, all except for the one central pair. My cuts are so swift and clean that the stumps seal over bloodlessly right before my eyes. Then I attach their severed feet all over my body; they suction themselves on as though they'd been designed to unite with my flesh.

But the strange thing is that I never Accelerate; unlike real-me, dream-me is happy to remain on the ground wiggling those multitudes of toes. In fact, instead of ascending the heights, she collapses into a low, prone, caterpillar-like position from which she gazes up at her sisters, who stand there bewildered, blinking.

"Let me take you on a tour through the sensations of Slow-World," she tells them. "There's so much you've been missing."

A Day's Work

I've been with TimeJaunt ever since they recruited me right out of grad school twenty years ago, and now I can't imagine working anywhere else.

My first position was in the therapy branch dealing with issues like Weltanschauung Contagion, which occurs when a client returns from the past saturated with an outmoded worldview (for instance, Ptolemaic cosmology); Phantom Absence Syndrome, in which a traveler's convinced they've left part of their soul in some previous century; and Constriction Nostalgia, a painful, paradoxical longing for the extinct sensation of life without loopbacks.

I also ran rehab groups for clients facing bankruptcy from their addiction to visiting various religions' miraculous events, as well as for their inverse soul-twins haunting history's horrors like pilgrims collecting anti-epiphanies. It's true that as you wander through the ages, you see inexplicable wonders and unendurable suffering—just like right now, of course, though it seems to pack more of an emotional wallop with chronotourism.

After a decade of those disorders, I was restless for change, so I applied for a lateral transfer. Now I'm a destination-events director, managing arrangements for clients who want to book a Walls-of-Jericho bar mitzvah, a Renaissance wedding, a

Viking-style burial for a loved one, etc. (as always, with travelers perceptible only to each other, not to the locals). I coordinate with the site facilitation teams that accompany excursions to forestall in-group brawls and scuffles—certain clients tend to flaunt a what-happens-in-the-past-stays-in-the-past attitude, and when you consider high blood alcohol levels and the pressure-cooker nature of those milestone family events, the need for these proverbial burly escorts is self-evident.

For the required outreach component of my job, I'm the company point person for the Eagle Scout quest—teens invisibly shadow pioneers and frontiersmen to acquire ancient skills, though farriery and blacksmithing are obsolete now, and why learn tracking when there's no more wilderness? (The Davy Crockett part of the package is a highly expurgated experience, set up to omit episodes like Crockett's savage bear-slaying exploits "over a thousand weight of fine fat bear-meat," as he infamously boasted.) And every Earth Day, I arrange the itinerary for the government-funded nationwide sixth-grade field trip to precolonial North America so that the next generation can behold living animals as well as actual trees, pristine waters, and clean, uncluttered sky, though most of the kids seem numb and vacuous, fingers twitching spasmodically, disoriented without their digital devices.

Though you'd assume that those of us in the entertainment venues—videographers, costume designers, and so on—would be the cheeriest, it's our linguists and philologists who behave as though history is a voluptuous cake they've been assigned to eat their way through with golden forks. Or you could say that they're like manic lepidopterists wielding their nets to capture miniscule instances of lexical shift. Our culinary workers, on the other hand, are always irritable about the logistics of transporting site-specific authentic meals cooked to our contemporary health standards; wherever you go in our hallways or on location, you glimpse them only through clouds of dry ice, though you can hear them muttering the choicest profanities of the ages.

New staffers are constantly debating the meaning of history— some of them even have a motto ("No point, no plot!"), while others argue that there must be some calculable teleology, but the rest of us don't see much difference between those two positions, just like underlining everything in a book is no different than leaving the entire text unmarked. And as for the question of free will, we've witnessed firsthand how actions and motivations are entangled across millennia; if such a thing exists, it must be very different from the self-contained moral mechanism of popular imagination.

That's why no one who's been here for more than a few years thinks much in narrative terms anymore; we feel claustrophobic watching movies or reading novels with their limited perspectives. And because we spend our social hours together, we're viewed as clannish, even elitist, but the truth is that we're at ease with each other's conversational elisions, and we never torment each other with questions like "How was your day?" or "What are you doing this summer?" since a day can be overlaid with many midnights, and a summer can include weeks of skating through a long-vanished Amsterdam December.

We've all learned the hard way that an overstay in our own chrono location causes an intense bodily agitation we call "the crawlies," so while in one sense we're the freest of humans because of the unlimited travel perk, in another we're the most constrained; we can't maintain equilibrium without frequently dipping into the time-stream, though our clients don't experience this because not even the wealthiest of them could afford our level of exposure.

We've even established sleep nooks at various nodes—I find it soothing to envision history as a honeycomb of secret stations, each climate-controlled to allow in just the right amount of chill while filtering out local pathogens. The Little Ice Age is the most popular, so refreshing compared to our own vastly overheated era.

It's a good thing we have our own retirement community, since after a full career here, no one could handle the social rhythms of a normal residential setup. But instead of holding forth with fantastic field anecdotes, our retirees are uncannily silent, which we always remark on after TimeJaunt reunions. Does frequent, prolonged immersion in the time-stream cause dissociation and aphasia so that in the wordless elders we're beholding what we'll become? Though we speculate about this in anxious whispers, no one ever quits. We're willing to pay the price of a constricted future for what we have now; with all its openings and passageways, its crannies and corners, the past is infinitely capacious.

Tune-up

But look, it's already time to call the Interventionist again! He shows up with his carryall neither a minute early nor a minute late.

"Good morning," he says, "How have things been going since the last checkup?"

"Pretty smoothly," says the mother, "except for the twins."

"Let's take a peek," he says as he slips out his spectralamp, so she calls the girls, positioning them a few inches apart, her hands firmly on their shoulders to keep them from squabbling or squirming.

As he switches on his lamp, aiming it at the empty air between them, shadow patterns appear on the floor, silhouettes of dense, knotted ropes twisting together in a roiling motion, edges sharp and distinct in the smoky blue light. The whole family watches in fascination, and the grandmother nods knowingly—as she frequently mentions, she herself would have become an Interventionist had the women of her day been allowed to train for public positions.

"Ah," he says. "The knots are as numerous as ever, but you can see where there's significant fraying here—" (he gestures with the mahogany tuning wand) "and core deterioration there. It's surprising to find that kind of damage in siblings this young, especially twins; this signifies intense personalities and consequential destinies. Looks like I'll have to do some restringing before I tune."

"No wonder there've been so many arguments and tears," says the mother.

The grandmother goes to the big cedar chest right next to where the Interventionist is standing and opens it, bending over painfully to reach in and draw out an invisible length of emergency cordage. "Is this enough?" she asks. "We've gotten low since all the work last year."

"No need to state the obvious," says the mother, a bit of a bite in her voice.

"It'll be fine, it's precisely the right amount," the Interventionist replies quietly, glancing away.

Taking a slender vial from the carryall, he pours a few drops of fizzy fluid into each of the two child-size tin cups the oldest sister holds out to him. The twins find the minty aroma appealing and drink eagerly, whining for more even as they collapse onto the carpet into a semisedated state.

The Interventionist sets up the spectralamp on its little tripod and kneels on the floor to lean over them, his three-dimensional hands weaving in and out of the shadows so swiftly that the other children become dizzy and have to sit down, though they can't seem to look away; no one ever tires of gazing at these projected manifestations of kinship bonds during those brief times they're visible.

"OK, that oughta hold it," says the Interventionist, leaning back on his heels after a few moments of intense work. The twins stir sleepily, then pull themselves up to sit, uncharacteristically subdued.

Now the others gather round them in a cluster for the family tuning, simple and routine. The lamp's angle is adjusted so the light can cover them all as the Interventionist rearranges fittings to reduce subtle strains, untangling the beginnings of gnarls and tightening knots just barely beginning to slacken, rubbing in a measure of aromatic shadow oil to smooth the weave and keep it supple; nobody likes dry, raspy, itchy connections.

After he's finished and the lamp is restored to the carryall, the Interventionist accepts the glass of ritual hospitality liqueur, then cordially bids them all farewell until next time. But as he strides away, he ponders their family history, the serious surgeries he performed in that household after the father's departure and the brother's death, all those splices and grafts using up so much of their supply of emergency cordage. It's situations like this that have eroded his faith in the very social structure he's sworn to sustain, yet he knows that it's not for him but for younger, braver guild members to plan in whispers, risking their vocations, even their lives, as they design a more equitable system for configuring the soul's rope.

Stretchies

In the neighborhood where I grew up, at least one member of each family had been CRISPR-ed to prolong their childhood. For some, this was permanent, as with the cherubic forever-three-year-old whose enormous face beamed at the world from promotional billboards everywhere, but most were programmed to eventually grow up after decades of remaining at the designated age.

Now, all these years later, no matter how well an adult stretchy thinks they're passing, the telltale signs are apparent. Some walk through the world dreamy and languid, as though an essential aggression or vehemence of spirit was smothered under countless cupcakes and play dates. Others exude an air of resentment; having regarded childhood as a state of enforced humiliation best gotten over with as quickly as possible, they'd experienced its artificial extension as a crime not just against nature but against their very souls. Still others are cynical to the core from observing the interactions of adults who didn't bother to maintain high standards in their presence, assuming they were too young to understand. Then there are those who couldn't outgrow their innocence; they're painfully forthright, unable to speak anything other than their immediate truth despite the social repercussions.

It's not that all the stretchies are shunned, now, exactly; the collective emotion seems to be pity-at-a-distance as the public tries to suppress their retroactive shame about this enterprise that was so widely celebrated at the time of its inception. With the stretchies' parents long gone, the permanent children in foster homes, and the ones who grew up scattered, struggling to blend in or languishing on society's margins, there's no "there" for me to return to even if I wanted to since I was never really one of them, though I don't quite belong in the "normal" world, either.

My sister was born two years after my brother, but they've functioned as twins for all but the first part of their lives since they were both set to remain at the age of seven (our mom's favorite stage: gap-toothed grins, tadpole pets, basic fractions, *James and the Giant Peach*).

That's why as I neared retirement age, I found myself still volunteering with my brother's Cub Scout troop and buying spangly pink nail polish for my sister to make her fingertips glitter as she performed roundoffs in Junior Gymnastics, even as I cared for my parents during their final illnesses. Of course, after having been burdened with my siblings' never-ending childhood, I never wanted kids of my own—now that I'm in what are supposed to be my own golden years, I wonder who'll look after *me* as I decline? I certainly can't count on the "twins"; they're still trying to learn skip counting and memorize the multiplication tables. And most importantly, after I'm gone, how will they adjust to life in foster homes?

These questions trouble me and the others in this same situation; during our Stretchy Sibs support group meetings, we try to talk it through—the frustration, the anxiety, and yes, the strange, humiliating envy . . . Our process isn't just about affirmations and shared tears, though; we have a cadre of lobbyists on Capitol Hill pushing for enhanced care for everyone involved; clearly, the powers that be have a lot to answer for since they failed to foresee that their bizarre social experiment would create a legion of orphans and untold legacies of displacement, all in the name of family values.

Genius Status

Though it's well past 1 p.m. when Myla arrives at the registry office to get her invention certified, registered, and named, no one's on duty at the information desk and all the cubicles are deserted. Looking around, she wonders—do the officials get a lengthy lunch break because they find it so exhausting to deal with all those applicants boiling over with ambition and mental schematics? Are there rows of cots in the basement for leisurely afternoon naps? She imagines public servants in sleep-rumpled uniforms stirring to check their watches, then burrowing into an even deeper slumber.

Having already taken two buses and a train to get there, she's not inclined to leave and come back later, so she takes her place at the end of the long line of inventors all side-eyeing each other with suspicion and hiding their creations—some under their jackets so it appears as though they're pregnant with irregularly configured offspring, others under tarps in wheelbarrows or dollies.

Myla's brainchild, however, clearly a biomechanical marvel, is naked in her arms, its tubes, wires, tentacles, plumes, and eyes exposed for all to see. Of course, the other inventors are ogling it, dying to know what it does, but inquiring would violate professional etiquette, so she enjoys watching them frown and murmur as they try to guess until at last she takes pity on them and lifts her device, turning it sideways to fully display its glory. "It's a device for flying out of the body. Who wants to try it?"

A clamor of vociferous volunteering echoes through the room. All of them want to go; unconstrained by physical limitations, they could visit every lab in the world, gathering ideas for future projects! But then, of course, they hesitate, realizing that whoever takes advantage of this offer won't be able to carry what they'd brought with them, risking intellectual property theft by those who remained behind.

"No problem," she tells them. "You can all leave your bodies at the same time as long as you're physically connected, so just make sure that one of you is touching the helmet wearer, and someone else is touching that person, and so on—you'll have to make a human chain. While you're traveling, I'll guard your inventions since I have to stay grounded to reel you back in."

"Can we trust her?" murmur the inventors. "She could abscond with our ideas while we're exploring! She could steal our fame!"

"Not a chance," she reassures them. "After what I've made, anything else would be anticlimactic. Besides, I'm not interested in fame."

"Not interested in fame?" The inventors are astonished. "Then why did you build this?"

"Just because," Myla says firmly. "Now do you want to travel or not?"

So, in just a few moments, they're all lying on the floor according to her instructions, holding hands as though they're outsized nursery schoolers on an imaginary sleeping-mat field trip. She crouches down to secure the detachable helmet on the head of the first person in line and presses the buttons in a rapid, complex sequence; the device coughs a few times to work up its concentration.

There's a prolonged hum, then a sustained whooshing sound as souls are sucked out through the pertinent portals, and suddenly Myla is alone in a sea of vacant bodies and shrouded and boxed inventions.

The inventors' physiques are either spindly or corpulent and their heads are notably on the large side; some of their open, staring eyes are crossed from having gazed too long at equations on their screens. Myla feels the weight of their collective earnestness so intensely that rather than aspiring to fly out of her own body, she longs to sink into it, and envisions the registry officers' subterranean lair— maybe one of them has recently retired without being replaced yet, so there's an extra bed with cool sheets and a downy pillow. But no, she can't abandon her post!

To keep herself awake, she eats the partially crushed cheese crackers languishing in their plastic casing in her backpack, then she jogs around the room, first clockwise, then counterclockwise. She does three sets of push-ups and awkwardly tries to reproduce the pirouettes of her elementary school ballet class years, but still, drowsiness threatens to overwhelm her. Finally, she entertains herself by taking the other inventions out of their containers and examining them. There's a mattress turner, a soup stirrer, a 100 percent silent pencil, a phone for sending aromas to friends and loved ones (the subtle bouquet of a vintage wine, the salt tang of the sea), a magnetic headset for time-stamping and recording thoughts and another for wiping out memories of book and movie plots so the user can repeatedly experience them for the first time. She's compiling a mental list of favorite films to delete from her hippocampus—should she start with *Alien* or *Blade Runner?*— when a side door opens and the registry officials begin to file in, yawning and rubbing their eyes.

"Well, well, what, what have we here?" asks the man with the supervisor badge as he surveys the prone inventors. "Did an electro-gravitational engine malfunction or was there a faulty anti-insomnia nebulizer explosion? It wouldn't be the first time!"

"No, sir," Myla explains. "These inventors just wanted to try my machine for flying out of the body, but I can bring them back for their interviews."

"No need, no need," says the supervisor hastily. "The process will be much more efficient if they remain comatose; this way, we won't even have to talk to them."

"But that's a complete short circuit of the application process!" Myla cries.

"Precisely!" says the supervisor, and gives a nod; immediately, the subofficers start sweeping through the room with their clipboards, giving each device in turn only a cursory glance as they check the boxes on their forms and assign names.

Myla's appalled—this goes beyond mere dereliction of duty; it constitutes grievous dishonor to the very spirit of innovation! She rushes over to the inventor in the helmet, drops down beside him, and starts turning dials and pushing buttons, her fingers flying as she activates the helical drive and initiates execution of the emergency soul-retrieval sequence. This time, instead of a whooshing noise, the sounds of many whistles being blown all at once fill the room as the inventors are yanked back toward their original dimensional coordinates, but in her haste, Myla has inadvertently transposed a few of the commands. The atmosphere, which until this point was aseptically bureaucratic, suddenly seems jangled, raw, and scorched as some of the inventors' souls touch down with a shock in the wrong bodies while others vibrate half-in, half-out of their own or hover just above them, unable to enter, all of them crying out for their mothers in their etheric voices with such urgency that their mothers have no choice but to appear, the living ones landing with a *thunk* in office or exercise attire, and the phantasmagorical ones floating halfway between the floor and ceiling in spectral versions of the outfits they were buried in and must spend their respective eternities wearing. Together, they constitute a throng, a multitude, a consternation of mothers, each of them peeved to have been so peremptorily summoned, all of them frowning as they assess the situation and roll up their fabric or ectoplasmic sleeves to get to work. Of course, they know precisely who belongs where, and no matter how bulky or asymmetrical an inventor's soul is, no matter how ill matched to its designated body it may be, any mother can knead it like bread dough and stretch it like taffy, manipulating it until it's stuffed back into its fleshy envelope.

Though this psychic process is shockingly violent, it lasts only a few moments. Soon the inventors are sitting up, looking around, struggling to orient themselves even as they beg to return to their journeys, but their mystic portals have just been expertly sealed by the mothers so that this can never ever happen again, not because they have anything against soul travel per se, but because they're loath to be interrupted in their worldly or extramundane pursuits by inane emergencies arising from their grown children's attempts to attain genius status as compensation for the terror of being vulnerable entities comprised of mostly empty space and electron clouds in an entropic, expanding universe.

Ravenously hungry from their exertion, the mothers are ready to hit the streets and descend upon whichever local buffet offers the most prodigious spread (the ghosts can quasi-satisfy themselves by suctioning in ocular impressions of food through their eyes).

"Myla," they call. "Come with us!"

"But I'm not a mother! And besides, my device hasn't received its name yet," Myla responds.

"You have brought something new into the world just for its own sake," says the oldest living mother, "which means it's yours to name."

Awe comes upon Myla. Having never had the opportunity to name a living entity, not even a goldfish or a gerbil, she immediately decides that she will dedicate her entire lifespan to this project, considering each possibility in every known language as well as aggregate names and novel synthetic names, deferring satisfaction until her very last breath when she'll gasp out the perfect choice.

Gathering up her device (which is growing larger even as it sprouts new tentacles aglitter with tiny hooks), she joins the surge of walking/floating mothers as they exit the building, leaving the sleep obsessed and the attention starved to console each other as best they can.

Reversals

Like infants accidentally switched at birth, sometimes cremation urns are sent to the wrong homes along with their accompanying ghosts.

If this error isn't discovered by the end of the first day, the arrangement can't be rectified since each ghost's essence has already begun to "set" in its new environment, no matter how mismatched; exchange attempts inevitably lead to phantasmal tantrums, putrid, pulsing miasmas in the breakfast room, and the like.

So that's where the support groups come in. The bereaved sit on folding chairs in a circle, urns on laps, ghosts flickering and strobing behind them while the counselors offer therapeutic tips on how to deal with spectral sleep disorders and disparities in domestic culture (for instance, when a ghost from a formal, reticent environment ends up with a family of partyers).

Only rarely does a ghost prefer the new arrangement to its original one, but when this turns out to be the case, even more trouble ensues; enraged that it wasted its previously embodied life with incompatible kin, the ghost tends to overcompensate by clinging so tightly to family members that they find it nearly impossible to go about their daily routines, and spend all their time rubbing their skin raw trying to scrape off the sticky ectoplasmic residue.

For this situation, any number of support groups would prove insufficient, so a team of specialists must descend upon the home to provide on-site coaching in afterlife individuation and boundary work. Sadly, the success rate of such interventions is moderate at best, and usually the team decamps after a month or so, declaring the case unresolvable.

At that point, all the family can do is smash the urn, bury its shards in a designated part of the cemetery, scatter the ashes, then move out of their house, not together, since the ghost would go with them, but individually, all the children and pets going to different relatives, and the parents taking separate apartments on opposite ends of town. This confuses the ghost, which tries to reach all of them at once, stretching its form like ethereal taffy—a shimmering foot here, a transparent hand there—until at last it pulls itself apart and dissipates. Though the family could return, they usually choose to relocate instead since no matter how vigorously they spray and scour, the house never gives up that telltale eerie ozone odor, almost as though it misses being haunted.

The House Sitter

Down the driveway they roll in reverse into the darkness, their car weighed down with luggage, the house behind them so audibly straining in its moorings that they have to crank up the windows and blast their music.

As the house bucks and shudders, the house sitter drums gently with her fingers on the furniture to soothe it. After a while, the house settles down to a low-level quivering that continues through the small hours of the morning, though the sitter doesn't let down her guard since she knows what's coming.

And indeed, by first light the house seems not only to have recovered its strength but to have adopted the stratagem of the python; slowly, at first, then with ever-increasing speed and intensity, the living room begins to contract, the walls closing in upon the house sitter as she holds her place, cross-legged and straight-backed in the center of the floor.

But the house sitter senses that this particular house is not, in fact, a killer. Oh, she's known killers before, and understands that there's a time when even the most seasoned professional must exit, flee to the registry, and sign to have the house put down; in this case, however, she senses no malice, just desperation seeping from the grains of the wood paneling and pooling invisibly along the baseboards, so not only does she maintain her position but she pretends to be oblivious to the fact that the walls are sweeping the heavy furniture toward her from every direction. To all appearances, she's simply enjoying a relaxed Sunday morning with the crossword on her phone. "Ort," she keys in as the oak entertainment system and the seven-foot-long couch nudges her. And "Hawaiian goose, that's 'nene,'" she murmurs, forcing the oxygen through her rib cage as the fabric of the couch impresses its pattern on her skin. And sure enough, it isn't long before she can feel the house hesitate, even sag a little. The room gives two more half-hearted squeezes, and soon the walls begin to expand again, the entire structure bested and maybe even spooked by her aplomb. She's careful to give no sign of personal satisfaction, thus allowing the house to save face. A true professional never humiliates their client.

Each house grieves for its owners in an individual way, so the sitter knows she has to be ready for anything as she feels the house brooding, taking her measure. All is calm and quiet for a while, but then suddenly, while she's making lunch, the kitchen begins to whirl in place like a child trying to make itself dizzy. The sitter smiles to herself; this is a beginner's device which a more experienced edifice would never deign to employ. Ignoring her sudden nosebleed, the house sitter digs her cleats into the floor, though lightly, so as not to cause startlement or pain, and leans in the direction of the spin like an Olympic luge runner steering their vehicle into a skid; the house, which was counting on her resistance, immediately loses its equilibrium and rocks to a halt.

Once more, the sitter doesn't allow any hint of victory to surface in her demeanor. She also takes pains to suppress the affection she's beginning to feel for her passionate, naive young charge; she must work hard to remain clinical, detached at every stage of the process. True, one hears occasional rumors of sitters who go rene-gade, seducing or being seduced by houses in their care, but these stories typically end in mutual immolation.

Before people learned that houses have souls, house sitting was merely a casual gig for impoverished grad students and budget-conscious travelers who tended to be hasty and inept as they man-handled their charges into submission. The sitter finds it painful indeed to think about all the generations of houses that suffered before this work was recognized as a noble vocation requiring a three-year training regimen (bloodshed, chanting, ordeals, and stra-tegically combined psychoactive substances). She's even more pro-tocol obsessed than her fellow graduates, since her desire to nurture houses springs directly from her childhood in the orphanage—it wasn't a terrible institution, and in fact, she even had some pleasant times there, but she was always grimly aware of her station in life. Now, however, the Sacred Guild is her family, and the houses are her beloved foster children.

By this point, she senses that the house is secure enough in her presence that she can putter around a little. She takes a quick shower in the guest bathroom. She plays the station the radio is set on even though she finds talk shows annoying. These activities provide the house with familiar sensations while it's in a becalmed state—if she'd attempted them before demonstrating her mastery, the house might have lost control of its systems in a frenzy from which nobody could have brought it back, but now it only gives only an initial shiver, then subsides into stillness. She even fiddles with the thermostat, but there's no eruption of rage in the form of an electrical surge or furnace explosion. From here on in, the sitter knows, as long as she remembers to tread lightly, respectfully, their course will remain smooth.

And so it goes for a while. Occasionally, the house vents a little spleen—one of the burners on the stove flickers out, or the smoke alarm squawks for no apparent reason, but she knows it's best to overlook these incidents. By the end of the first week, both house and sitter are mostly sleeping through the night.

Now that the house has let down its guard, the sitter can begin to get to know its ways on a deeper level. Before showing up on the premises, she studied the informational packet containing specs of the electrical, plumbing, and HVAC systems, but as she settles into occupancy, she becomes aware of its gradations of density and texture, the tonal shifts of its hummings, dimmings, brightenings, and creakings. And she senses that the house is learning her, too, not just as its keeper but as a fellow organism vulnerable to aches, hunger, itches, fatigues, and microelations; an undercurrent of intimacy grows with the most delicate kind of indirection and mutual shyness, every interaction understated, every glance sidelong. Almost before they've noticed, autumn is arriving.

It's at some point in the midst of the seasonal gutter cleaning, leaf-raking, and chimney checking when she first starts to notice some low-level anomalies—an unpredictable structural twitch or spasm, not in pique, but seemingly idiopathic, an occasional sour gust drifting through the ventilation system, apparently with no particular source. She decides to watch and wait before calling in the Guild doctors. Maybe the house is simply off its feed because the sky has been sullenly withholding sunshine and rain—this weather's sure to change before too long, providing proper nourishment.

But then the kitchen door starts to stick as though it's catching on something, just a little at first, then increasingly, until late one afternoon she finds it almost impossible to open. She exits through the front door, then walks around the yard, approaching the kitchen door from the outside. To her shock she finds that the threshold is a full half inch below a little ledge of earth.

She looks for a long moment, then goes back around the house, assessing the situation—it's just as she fears—the high basement windows have started to slip down; the entire house is gradually but visibly beginning to sink.

Perspiring despite the slight chill, she hurries back in and takes the basement stairs two at a time though there's no need for haste since she already knows what she'll find. Yes, there in the northern corner, the cement floor has thinned and softened to translucence, turning to gel.

She climbs the stairs, slowly this time, and sits on the porch steps, then immediately jumps up and begins to pace the flagstones, nearly nauseous with rage, not needing to check for the other signs since the situation is clear: this house is very ill, with probably only a few months left. There would have been, of course, other more subtle diagnostic indicators before her arrival, but instead of arranging for palliative care, the owners had patched, spackled, painted, and decorated over them, then pretended to go off on an ordinary trip, abandoning their house to the care of a sitter since it's illegal to leave any house without a human to tend it. They have no intention of returning; the house sitter doesn't have to try their emergency number to know that it's fake.

Poignantly, the house itself must be unaware of its situation since the disease presents insidiously in its initial painlessness, inducing a false sense of cheer and well-being even as the foundation begins to liquify. The final weeks, however, are always brutal, with fevers and chills, respiratory distress, and the violent seizure that precede collapse. Not only have the owners failed to provide the house the necessary season of spiritual preparation for its death ordeal, but they've left it in the hands of a stranger just when it most needs nurturing by those who have known it since its infancy.

Her immediate impulse is to report them, but by the time all the administrative and procedural requirements can be completed, the owners will have fully settled into their new identities, quite unlocatable. She could leave right away, try to pick up their trail in order to hunt them down and administer vigilante vengeance, but she'd have to forsake the house, leaving it to suffer alone. On the other hand, if she waits until the house dies and then observes the 101-day ritual mourning period, it'll surely be too late to find them. Despite its rigor, her education has left her completely unprepared for this impossible choice between justice and responsibility.

But she can't pace the flagstones for much longer or the house will begin to suspect that something's amiss—she must protect its innocence. While she tries to come up with a plan, she'll have to construct a dense emotional shield, though this might in itself alert the house, so the thing to do is distract it. Laboriously cloaking her thoughts in blandness, she goes inside and moves from room to room switching on every television, a rare treat guaranteed to immediately throw the house into a thrill of confusion. Then she makes herself a gin and tonic and goes upstairs to stretch out on the master bed though up until now she's dutifully slept only in the guest room.

Hours later she's awakened in the dark by a gentle, insistent tapping in the crook of her outflung arm. Her heart thumps almost audibly and her mind churns, but she manages to keep herself from startling, and maintains a slow, steady breathing pattern, pretending she's still asleep as she runs through the most obvious possibilities—there's been a break-in; the owners have repented and returned; there's a visiting relative with a key. Of course, she's always faithfully kept the doors locked at night, and the house itself would have already alerted her to the presence of any intruders—besides, why would a burglar want to wake her, especially with such a mild, even tender touch? As for the owners, they're clearly gone for good, and according to the contract, she would have been informed ahead of time about any visitor. No, there can be only one explanation. Without moving her head, she cracks open one eyelid, just a slit, barely enough to peer through, and stifles a gasp—it's just as she'd thought.

After taking a moment to center herself as she mentally runs through the pertinent aspects of her training, she opens her eyes to fully behold the child gazing at her—small, naked, luminously pale almost to the point of transparency, with a shock of white-blond hair like downy feathers. It is the soul of the house, one hand holding a burning candle, the other doing the tapping.

A house's soul manifests itself to humans only in extreme circumstances and always unpredictably. For instance, there was the textbook case of the house with the sparrow that swooped from room to room in warning, disappearing only after the occupants checked all their systems and discovered the carbon monoxide leak. There was the renovator who had to scoop out a debilitated house's soul in the form of rotten pumpkin seeds from a declivity in the back garden. But when a house's soul manifests as a bee colony inside the walls, the family cherishes the heat, the humming, and the sweet fragrance because they know some extraordinary event will occur that year—an unexpected financial windfall, perhaps, or a life-changing epiphany, or the birth of a child with a lofty destiny.

Manifestation in human form, however, is rare because it signifies that the soul is preparing to vacate the premises on a journey of its own, leaving the house an empty shell. Of course, a house soul on the loose is an unnatural state of affairs—as soon as it's reported, the Guild Police releases an APB, and an Apparition Alert pops up on everyone's phone.

Since the appearance of this child constitutes a spiritual emergency of the highest order, the house sitter is legally obligated to summon the Guild SWAT team with its sirens, lights, bullhorns, soul-sniffing hyenas, and a battalion of mages, sealing off the premises and relentlessly performing rituals to force body and soul back together. There are severe penalties for noncompliance, the least of which is immediate expulsion from the Guild. She reaches for her phone, but then hesitates, feeling an almost physical pang at the prospect of consigning this house to the Guild's painful ministrations and then numbing her heart so she can move on to another job.

That's when the child leans in to press her forehead gently against the house sitter's, communicating through a jumble of images, a strange telepathic patois, that it's known about its condition all along, and has only been waiting for her to discover it.

The house sitter is disoriented, a little dizzy, because the house soul's thoughts and emotions don't seem alien to her; instead, they're strangely familiar, as though the spiritual DNA of humans and houses is more similar than the Guild is willing to acknowledge—or maybe all the abandoned of the earth are true and rightful kin.

But she also feels a great relief; now the two of them can leave together, since unensouled, the house will immediately lose consciousness, experiencing no pain as it gradually succumbs to its illness. In the gap between the moment they walk out the door and the moment when the physical structure releases its final breath and the house soul, by then miles away, passes into the afterlife, there will be just enough time for them to follow the delicate etheric thread that still connects the house soul to the fugitive owners, just enough time to exact vengeance. All disincarnate entities have significant powers at their disposal, so reprisal will be epic, well worth the penalty of damnation.

But when the portal to everlasting banishment opens, the house sitter won't let the child step through alone; she'll squeeze in with it, ready to take her place as the only human in the hell of homes that have violated the sacred statutes in one way or another.

Even now in her mind's eye she can picture all those exiles arrayed across that vast and desolate plain, waiting for her to console them.

Donations

No one ever refuses his request.

"Of course!" each stranger says immediately, as though terrified he'll change his mind. "Yes, please take my shame!"

And then they reach inside to scoop it out like quivering gobs of rancid chicken fat, unseen yet palpable, and plop it into his wheeled forty-five-pound weatherproof airtight pet-food storage container, the handiest transport system he could come up with.

Is he a masochist or martyr, planning to haul all that shame into his kitchen, fry it up and gobble it down? Is he an installation artist preparing to wrap the city in a heavy blanket of shame as an ideological statement? No one knows, and they're too busy enjoying their freshly unclogged state to ask.

But it's not long before they need to track him down. He isn't hard to find—he's hermetically sealed himself within the invisible igloo-shaped structure made entirely of shame he's slathered together, packed down, and smoothed by hand from the inside. They can see him lounging serenely in his recliner.

"Give us back our shame!" they cry. "We don't know who we are anymore because we can't feel who we used to be!"

Sensing the presence of that great crowd all around him, he looks up—these donors must have gathered to convey their thanks, he thinks, or maybe they've already accumulated even more shame to offer, but he doesn't need it now that he's created his 100 percent insulated home. Previously, he worked with a range of structures and materials—cellulose, fiberglass, mineral wool, polyurethane, spray foam, caulk, epoxy, and radiant barriers—until he finally realized that all he needed was sufficient quantities of shame, not dredged from his own experiences, but from the psyches of others with whom he has no personal connection, so for him, the substance is neutral, inert, without any feeling tone whatsoever.

Grateful, he gives his visitors an awkward imitation of the queen wave he saw once on TV and has always wanted the opportunity to perform.

Relics

No one looks forward to harvesting a harp, but on the first anniversary of a death, the family trudges together to the cemetery, shovels in hand.

It's not just the labor of displacing all that earth that's so disturbing, or the eeriness of unsealing the coffin and slicing open the corpse's protective sheath so you can reach in with your gloved hand to pluck the harp from its nesting place just over the heart, but the uncanny nature of the instrument itself. A fist-size bony protuberance, it's not bone, cartilage, or desiccated sinew, but something like soul residue, a concrescence of the deceased's memories, at least insofar as anyone can determine.

Everyone knows that it's forbidden to make skin contact with the harp or play it, even shielded by your ceremonial gloves—not that you'd be inclined to do so, any more than you'd want to caress a loved one's internal organs. No, you slip it into the designated blue silk sack and take it home to uncover and hang in your garden, then bide your time as you wait for its awakening, though there's often a long indeterminate stage during which it may be only feigning somnolence.

Eventually, though, it always comes to, initially retaining its inwardness, refusing to make a sound; during this stage, be sure to avert your eyes whenever you walk by—give it time to acclimate to the loss of its coffin privacy. In the expansiveness of light and open air, it begins to unclench, releasing those first tentative tones you must make a show of ignoring as you nonchalantly clip the hedges or sweep the stoop lest the harp startle, succumb to its reticence, and fall silent forever. Instead, it must overhear itself gradually and inadvertently as though barely apprehending the melody, then little by little, it can begin to get used to its song until at last it allows the music to flow unimpeded.

Then the whole family gathers beneath the harp. Depending on how this experience unfolds, they might express grief, bewilderment, and even anger: *This music's not what we'd expected; why did she live among us as a stranger?* The opposite outcome is just as tragic: *No surprises here—the notes seem all too familiar, as though he was squeezed into his role.* Usually, though, the song embodies a combination of the unpredictable and the fondly known; family members respond with astonished gasps to some passages and sighs of recognition to others. And everyone secretly wonders, *What will my own song be like?* as they experience a mixture of grief and relief that they'll never know.

Of course, no garden hosts only a single harp; the breezes coax out shifting harmonies from generations of instruments swinging lightly from the branches. Listeners find even the occasional dissonance satisfying: *Those two never did get along,* one might murmur affectionately. *Things are just as they always were.*

That's why everyone scorns the family that left their grandmother's coffin above ground during the crucial year to spare themselves the labor of excavation; they should have known the body would turn out to be harpless since it requires the pressure of the soil squeezing the coffin on all sides to cook the instrument.

What a sad place their garden has become as they huddle together, trying to occupy the gap in the sound.

The Pillow Museum

Most people find a trip to the pillow museum so exhausting that afterward they need a long nap to recover from experiencing all the dreams the display items have absorbed from their original sleepers.

Theoretically, anyone could navigate the museum according to taste, steering clear of, for instance, the homicide pillow, the fetish pillow, and the arson pillow, as well as the pillows of Arnold Schoenberg, Charles Manson, and all those dental hygienists and IRS attorneys. Theoretically, one could choose only the pillows of the confectioner, the Olympic surfer, the dolphin whisperer, and so on, but nobody does this, since it's common knowledge that every shunned pillow takes offense, vengefully suctioning out a single breath from the visitor's lifespan as they pass it by on the microsleep tour—a tiny, insignificant portion until you start adding up all the individual penalties over the years.

Nevertheless, not only does everyone return frequently, especially when hosting out-of-town guests (the museum is our only tourist attraction), but most of us are employed here as well, sanitizing, repairing, plumping, positioning, and working as docents or gravity adjusters. Then, too, there are also the soothers, wakers-and-shakers of visitors, members of the custodial, managerial, and administrative staffs, and the guards who protect the pillows from theft and vandalism.

I've spent my entire working life at the museum, beginning in my teens as a lowly turner, then moving up to plumping and gravity work, and proceeding through the ranks until at the august age of fifty, I became acquisitions chief, which necessitates much travel as I follow the leads sent in by our field operatives all over the world. Though I've had to familiarize myself with many languages and cultures, the most arduous to acquire are the pillows' own dialects: layer upon delicate layer of sighs, exhalations, and silences. And because so many of the most obvious acquisitions had already been obtained before my tenure, this work is more demanding for me than it was for my predecessors who brought in the myriad of homespun pillows where George Washington laid his head, the astronaut pillows of Apollo 11, and so on.

It's fallen to me to track down esoteric, out-of-the-way treasures—the very first pillow, made of Mesopotamian stone, whose purpose was solely to raise the head above ground level, keeping insects from creeping into the ears and nose of the sleeper; a pair of ancient and costly Chinese jade matrimonial pillows; the crude straw pillow that cradled Marie Antoinette's preseveredhead in her loathsome prison; and my most recent procurement, Mata Hari's collapsible jet-black mulberry-silk pillow which she kept in her reticule—inside it still nestles the rare Kolibri pistol, antique even then, affectionately known as "the hummingbird" due to its diminutive size, only 2.7 millimeters, effective only at the most intimate of ranges.

Each potential candidate must be evaluated in its original habitat, though a pillow thus disturbed is likely to prove surly and taciturn at first, refusing to reveal the dreams it harbors. Some pillows even turn violent, but with my prowess in advanced pillow wrangling, I've never met one I couldn't eventually examine and subdue for transport. Strapped into an airplane seat, even the most recalcitrant captive settles and cools as it subtly preens itself, practically purring, since being in the air makes any pillow feel at peace in its own essence, flight undoubtedly reminding it of the suspension of sleep.

I myself live pillowless at home; I've assimilated so much of the pillows' inner lives (spending weeks with each of them at their origin sites rather than undergoing the mere three-minute sleeps allotted to museum visitors), it would be abusive to subject any pillow to the contents of my brain. Over time, I've grown used to my perpetual migraines and stiff neck, the long, uncushioned cramp as I torment myself with this question: If the museum were to go up in flames, and I had time to grab only one pillow, which would I rescue? Is there some objective scale by which to measure the worth of each?

It's only recently I've realized that the ultimate pillow is one we don't possess and can't acquire since it doesn't yet exist, though I've glimpsed it during moments of half sleep. It is the Pillow of the Future, that universal treasure no acquisitions chief will have to wander the world seeking since it'll be present everywhere, swathing each head as a luminous, porous, transparent bubble spun from consciousness itself—in fact, it will be visible even in fetal ultrasounds, a flexible, floating penumbra that contracts around the skull for passage through the birth canal, then blossoms outward with the first breath. Perhaps this pillow will hold whatever metamind humanity grows into, or perhaps it will be made of time or the music of the spheres—I can only speculate.

Then the Pillow Museum, if it still stands, will serve as a relic of our benighted era, where people's thoughts are still trapped inside their heads. School children will wander through the exhibit halls between rows and rows of permanently somnolent, empty pillows as their teachers say, *Think of it ... all those sleepers dreaming alone together!*

The Blue Telephone

Not even once in her many years did Mamma take any of the twelve sleep-replacement pills issued by the government to each citizen on their twenty-first birthday. Instead, she toughed out every crisis the old-fashioned way (catnaps, caffeine, splashes of cold water on the face), and then there'd be that long catch-up period afterward with silk eye masks and everyone tiptoeing around the house. Her daughters could never figure out whether she was taking a private moral stance against the interventions of science in natural processes, keeping the pills back for some ultimate emergency, or saving them to bequeath to her heirs, which was, in fact, the result of her lifelong abstinence, whatever her motivation might have been.

"Why didn't she sell just one of them on the stealth market and take that cruise she always talked about?" wonders the generous daughter as they stand there in Mamma's bedroom gazing at the bubble pack of pills on top of the nightstand.

"Screw the cruise," says the tough-minded daughter. "If she knew she wasn't going to take them herself no matter what, she could have used them to pay for all the grandchildren's college and postgrad. That's what we should do now, wipe out those student loans."

The prudent daughter frowns. "You know Mamma wasn't a stealth market kind of gal. No, we need to put them in the safe. Remember how Ashley had such a tough time right after the twins were born? If it hadn't been for my pills plus hers, she probably would have had to be hospitalized. Who knows what else will come up? We're a big family. Things happen."

The secretive daughter doesn't say anything since not only does she want them for herself but she's a clandestine member of Eyes Wide Open, the worldwide guerrilla movement to make the pills limitlessly available, effectively doubling the human lifespan from the inside out by giving everyone access to all that time wasted in slumber.

The youngest daughter shakes her head. "Everyone knows that the dead are more forthcoming than the living," she says. "We need to summon the Blue Telephone and find out what she wants."

The other sisters stare at her. "We get ONE conversation of 179 seconds," hisses the prudent daughter. "We need to wait, let the questions emerge over the years so we can prioritize. If we blow our opportunity now, we'll spend the rest of our lives kicking ourselves."

"The Blue Telephone!" says the generous daughter. "It's the perfect solution!"

The tough-minded daughter frowns. "There's no point in call-ing Mamma—we're here, she's not, so it doesn't matter what she'd say. If we don't take advantage of how prices are trending, we'll be eating that lost opportunity for generations!"

The youngest daughter presses her case. "But there are so many other things we could ask her, too, like who's Monica's baby daddy, and what's the secret ingredient for the goulash."

The tough-minded daughter scoffs. "It's bergamot for the gou-lash, just the tiniest trace. And you don't have to be a rocket scien-tist to be able to see that it's Alec."

"Of *course*, it's Alec, that's old news," says the generous daughter. "But Mamma used ground-up star anise, I'm sure of it because she always kept it hidden behind all the other spices, and when I told her last year that I was onto her, she just smiled and didn't say anything,"

"That means nothing," says the prudent daughter. "She *always* smiled and kept her lips sealed. It was her MO. No, I'd put my money down on smoked paprika. But it couldn't be Alec; Monica always goes for the bad boys, not the sweet ones."

The generous daughter says, "We owe it to Mamma to ask—so many unused pills, that's unheard of!"

"If she cared," says the tough-minded daughter, "she'd have mentioned it in her will."

The generous daughter shakes her head. "She drew up that will and forgot about it long before the pills were even invented."

"The phone call's not going to happen," says the prudent daughter. "Not yet, anyway. It wouldn't be right unless we all agreed."

Suddenly, they feel it—that shimmer in the air behind them! Turning in unison, they behold the Blue Telephone glowing atop the tufted chenille duvet.

The four sisters stand there frozen for a moment, as though stunned by its sapphire splendor, then look around at each other.

Then, "You bitch!" says the prudent daughter to the youngest daughter. "I can't believe you performed the summoning before we were ready!" She bursts into tears.

"I didn't, I swear!" says the youngest daughter. She turns to the generous daughter. "It was you, because you knew they'd blame me, and you could hide behind your perfect reputation, but I see through you, I always have!"

But the tough-minded daughter is uncharacteristically speechless, staring not at the phone, but at the nightstand—the pills are gone.

And where is the secretive daughter?

Accustomed to ignoring her, they hadn't noticed when she enacted the summoning ritual silently behind their backs, then took advantage of the shock of the phone's arrival to slide the pills into her pocket and slip out the door.

They hear her motorbike peeling away just as the Blue Telephone starts to ring.

Dear Oracle,

I've never sought relationship help from even an ordinary advisor before, let alone from someone like you, so I apologize for any awkwardness on my part as I mindspeak with you through the brain port.

I want to make it clear that I have no interest in the raging public debate about whether this circuitry connects supplicants with an AI, a human in a digital workplace on the other side of the world, or some kind of hybrid entity in a lab deep underground; whatever you are, algorithm or flesh and blood, I need some wisdom!

My problem is that I'm in love with a guy who's everything I'd never even dared to dream I could find in a mate and who feels the same about me. This isn't an unseasoned relationship; in our five years as a couple, we've been through the proverbial thick and thin together, and our commitment is stronger than ever. Our only obstacle is this: while my pedigree is pure, his family has a whole slew of death defectives on the patrilineal side. Of course, the actual numbers are a closely guarded secret, and due to the stigma, I wouldn't dream of broaching the subject with his parents, but as far as we can ascertain, his grandfather is no more than 11 percent dead and his three great-uncles hover somewhere in the low-to-mid twenties. Further back, there's just silence and a family cemetery whose gravestones bear only female names in varying degrees of legibility.

Because of this, my little cohort of best friends has been relentlessly advising me to run like hell; last week they even ambushed me with an intervention.

"Do you want to spend the rest of your life picturing him being escorted onto the relocation train because he's failed to accomplish an expeditious death?" they asked. "Not to mention any sons you might have! And what if something terrible happens, God forbid—imagine them as undying disease or accident victims forever in exile!"

"The relocation centers offer mortality therapy," I protested weakly, but of course, they scoffed, and considering the abysmal success rate, I wasn't inclined to press that point.

Despite what most people assume, it's clear to me that this is a genetic, not a moral, flaw; he isn't one of those slackers who claims to be a natural-born death maven ready to just wing it when the time comes, and then fails to their everlasting shame. (I'll never understand that mentality—what kind of a world would this be if death just happened of its own accord without anybody taking personal responsibility for it?) No, he conscientiously complies with the training protocol; each morning he performs not only the standard meditations and visualizations but the advanced bodywork as well, including all twelve levels of pneumatic introjection. He's completely committed to the lonely, arduous exertion required to coax one's nascent death from the infinitesimal seedpod nestling between the kidney and the spleen and then to prevent it from retracting, shriveling, shrinking back—to force it instead to coil and burgeon, millimeter by voluptuous millimeter, through all the body's conduits until the process is complete, ready to blossom in the fullness of time and at the appropriate occasion.

Oh, it's so unfair—if not for that sole hereditary flaw, he could surely achieve the honorable death he deserves instead of being destined to turn into a partially expired freak with a cold, heavy hand or foot or a moribund head or elbow, and everything else still humming with vitality!

Of course, we've talked about trying to get him on a death-transplant list, either legitimately or through the black market via some cash-strapped citizen's illicit backroom deathectomy, but that's just an exercise in frustration as neither of us is independently wealthy or exorbitantly salaried; we're just ordinary workers with aging vehicles, corner-shop haircuts, and decades of student loan debt still ahead of us. Nevertheless, compared to some well-heeled couples we've seen whose faces are glazed over with mutual indifference, we're rich beyond all calculation; the thought of each of us going our separate ways in hopes of finding a "better" match is nauseating. What we have is irreplaceable; we must find a way to stay together at any cost!

At any cost, yes—even now, I feel my anterior superior temporal gyrus sparking with understanding as it dawns on me that since we can't change *his* situation, any hope of a shared future rests entirely on me—there's only one thing I can do, and it's drastic indeed. During the very next Morning Observances, instead of nurturing my personal death, urging and enticing it to grow within me, I'll slash at its tender stalk, rip off its shoots, leaves, and buds no matter how agonizingly it shrieks. It's true that the more well-cultivated a death is, the hardier it's likely to be, but I'm confident that I can prevail. Though the thought of violently desecrating this most intimate lifelong companion is chilling, I'd rather experience the trauma of enacting that mutilation in order to share my beloved's condition than resign myself to living without him.

As I ponder my plan, I can see that the hardest part will be the secrecy, especially since we've never kept anything from each other. Despite the fact that if our positions were reversed, he'd certainly make the very same choice, it would be disastrous for me to tell him what I'm going to do. First, he'd beg me to change my mind, then he'd awkwardly, endearingly, and ineffectually "forbid" me to go through with this, and finally, he'd try to bring the full force of the law down upon me to protect me from my own intention. No, I have to bear the weight of this decision alone; I can tell him only when my death is already shredded, bleeding, and silent within me.

Of course, dear Oracle, I gratefully acknowledge that these insights are produced by electrical impulses flowing through the brain port to boost my cognitive abilities in conjunction with my deepest values. Indeed, this session has been more than worth all those months of scrimping on groceries and foregoing coffee-shop outings and date nights to scrape up enough money for fifteen minutes worth of ideation enhancement, but surely my time is up and my designated attendant will be here momentarily to disconnect me! She must be running late; I couldn't help but notice how busy the Center is today, with a seeker of one sort or another in every chair, all those crystal headsets glistening. Please don't misunderstand me—I'm not complaining. I assume I won't be charged for this additional time. Even though I'm starting to get a bit of a migraine; I'll just try to relax by envisioning my future with the man I love, our home, our children—

But I'm galvanized; I can feel my skull buzzing as I realize that all of this can be about so much more than just the two of us! I can see the big picture, I can envision the sweep of history and my place in it; instead of keeping my deathicide a secret, I'll boldly announce it on social media, and this tale of transgressive passion will go viral within the hour, creating a crack in our ossified social structure. Then other death defectives and their loved ones will gather courage to band together and speak out instead of hiding, trying to pass, or squandering their resources on crank cures. And allies will rise up as well, the moral outrage surging like a mighty tide as more and more of the population questions the protocols, the banishments, the entire setup, demanding reform. Just think of the upheaval, an entire generation of mortality police decommissioned and retrained, sent out to lead the exiles home!

But Oracle, why are there suddenly all these sirens and flashing lights?—I'd assume that there's been some minor incident, an electrical fire in one of the consultation chambers, perhaps, but I don't smell anything burning, so this must be just a routine safety drill. I do see quite a few attendants purposefully heading my way, no doubt to apologize for the delay, disconnect me, and escort me to the post procedure lounge where I'll sip fruit juice and key in a five-star review for you on my tablet. Considering all you've done for me, it's the very least that I can do.

The Underlife

As my friends Naomi and Natalie observed their older cousins struggling with the logistics of bras and sanitary equipment, they made a pact with each other in their secret twin language to forgo the entire experience of womanhood, thus establishing themselves as the Bartlebys of preadolescence.

Decades later, in their hot early thirties, strolling together through the mall behind a woman with wrinkly elbows and orthopedic shoes, they whispered to each other that there'd be no way they'd ever let themselves get like that; it took them both a moment to realize they'd been speaking in their old language risen from the depths of disuse solely for this vow.

*

We like to ask my friend Alina, the animal psychic, how it feels to make contact with nonhuman consciousness.

"I've noticed more of a distinction between wild-mind and the minds of domestic animals than between domestic animals and their humans," she says.

"What are wild thoughts like, then?"

"Spiky in places, but much less anxious than tame ones."

Though we continue to press her, she can't, or won't, elaborate.

*

Deep in unremitting January, my nervous friend Amy pulls on her boots for a calming snowy trespass. Her destination: the neighbor's farm where his bees are wintering. From her coat pocket she pulls out her thrift-store stethoscope, places the diaphragm against the hive wall, and listens, humming along with the bees as they flex their wing muscles repeatedly at great speed to warm the cluster that shelters the queen at its heart. After a while, she begins to feel her mind slipping into equilibrium in much the same way that decades ago, during an entirely different life stage, the full-throttle sensory overwhelm of New York city streets counterbalanced her agitation as the quiet pastureland she'd grown up in couldn't do. Sometimes the hive's song sounds atonal, other times it hovers around A-sharp.

*

A woman as hard-pressed as my friend Shira (two jobs, three daughters) needs a secret to keep her afloat, so she's had one for years—not an affair, not a hidden bank account, not fentanyl pilfered from the medical supply cabinets at the hospital where she works third shift, not even gourmet chocolates in her pockets, but her obsession with cryptic pregnancies, the exact opposite of phantom pregnancies.

That's why despite her fatigue, on her nights off she binges on reruns: all four seasons of *I Didn't Know I Was Pregnant* (also those extra episodes about women who have experienced this twice, *I Still Didn't Know I Was Pregnant*).

In line at the post office or filling her shopping cart at Walmart, she glances surreptitiously at everyone around her, speculating about who might be in just this condition, though it's not the expectant ones she envies but their inhabitants, each suspended in serene anonymity.

*

Ever since my friend Mercedes learned that instead of making your bed in the morning, you should pull down the top sheet and blankets, exposing the bedding to kill dust mites, whenever she feels jittery as she moves through the city, she pictures her bed breathing alone as it basks in the light surging in through the window.

*

Over the years, three of Solange's friends, diarists all, have told her that they've invented private punctuation marks, notations for subtle, untranslatable emotions and gaps in feeling (*All numbnesses are not identical*, one explains); two have even told her they've included her in their wills, bequeathing her their journals.

But she doesn't want to read about their romances, their ambitions, their family strife, their musings and grievances, or even their favorite meals; all she wants to see is those pages magically expunged of everything *but* the marks, like traces of tracks on a snowy field after the birds have flown.

*

My friend Charlotte has placed a miniature replica of her home (same white timber frame, same porch, same gable windows) in the midst of her chickens. They strut and peck around it like benignly incompetent tutelary spirits, their footfalls jolting hypothetical scaled-down versions of Charlotte and her family, who undoubtedly regard these looming presences with aplomb—poultry as weather, just an ordinary local condition.

*

Moving from the West Coast to the East in order to develop a relationship with deciduous trees, my friend Cheryl gave up redwood spires sipping fog in silence, a horizon indistinguishable from the Pacific's most extreme visible blue, and the experience of staying drunk on hyperclarified light. During that cross-country drive, her pets in carriers and her furniture in tow, she felt the faint memory traces of her ancestors, their disappointment in her as they headed in the opposite direction.

*

It so happened that my friend Leslie was touring Notre Dame on the very morning of the fire. When asked later, *What was it like?* she says, *Like religion itself. Kind of cluttered, but kind of spacious, too, with something smoldering just beyond my awareness.*

*

Though it's been nearly six months since my friend Mattie died suddenly and unexpectedly, her apartment remains vacant. Watering her abandoned garden now, I remember her telling me that during the four years she lived on a houseboat with her then-husband, when the hose they used for spraying the deck got too knotted to work with, they'd drop it by one end into the ocean, where it instantly became so malleable that it disentangled itself. She told me also about the custom of water burial, mixing the deceased's ashes with concrete in a bucket, then attaching a radio beacon so you can return to that one spot in the vast unmarked graveyard of the sea.

*

On my friend Joanne's first day of school in America, they tried to teach her how to pledge allegiance to the flag, but she declined because in her previous school when she'd lifted her arm to heil Hitler as usual, the teacher, blanching, had hissed, *Nein, nein,* though not long before that, *everyone* had heiled Hitler each morning, so clearly, grown-ups were constantly changing their minds about these things, and she wasn't going to fall for it anymore.

*

It's 1988. My friend Mary and I are in her yard with our children. Glimpsing the flash of a blue jay's tail high in the pine, her son pulls back his bowstring and sends his blunt toy arrow into the branches where it catches. He shoots a second arrow to try to knock it down, and then another and another until his quiver is empty, all the arrows stuck out of reach. Looking up at the tree, we stand there in silence for a long time inside the sensation of time pressing down upon us even as it speeds impersonally away.

*

My friend Nina's treatment for a rare, aggressive cancer requires the suppression of all her immunities and the introduction of a stranger's stem cells into her bone marrow. Since her donor is male, Nina frequently ponders the fact that if she's ever murdered, her body hidden somewhere, the police will search for a male corpse due to the witness of the blood all over the crime scene.

*

In her much younger years my friend Sandra dated the man who created the most famous outdoor adventure/education program in the world. At that time, if your guy was into something, you had to be into it, too, which is why she found herself rappelling alone from a helicopter with only a compass, a box of waterproof matches, and a knife. During the week it took her to make her way back to civilization, she lost ten pounds; she remembers being so hungry that she cut off the head of a fish she'd caught by hand and bit into its flesh, its lungs still pumping.

In what sense is it accurate to speak of the raw-fish-devouring Sandra, the interim Sandra of the black cowboy hat and leopard-print stiletto-heel shoes, and the current Sandra, quiet caregiver of her aged mother, as the same woman?

*

Is having an uncontainable secret the closest a man can come to being pregnant? wonders my friend Barbara.

*

My friend Laura's life theory is that the first few sips of coffee are always the best: bright bitterness with frothy swirls of cream delivering a direct hit to the brain's pleasure center. And with the last few as well, she's all attention, everything cooling now in sweet potency like a receding tide—it's almost over, it's over, it's aftertaste to savor.

But the middle? It's lost in conversation, in message checking, in mind wandering, in work. Isn't it this way with everything from tiramisu to kisses?

That's why Laura fantasizes about excising that entire in-between territory

Hello Americano pour-over, hello crème brûlée smartly cracked open by the spoon, hello new love.

Then immediately, goodbye final sip, final bite, poignant last embrace.

She was fully present for all of it.

She didn't miss a thing.

*

No matter the amplitude, the buoyancy, the layered colors and lights, not one of my friends enjoys an easy coexistence with her hair.

*

All my friends and I dream of lost babies and toddlers—approximately grape-size, hidden somewhere in a tangle of sheets and blankets, for instance, or alive and unfed for months in a room no one knew was there. *They're the children we didn't conceive*, says one friend. *No, they're our actual children we worry about*, says another. *They're really versions of ourselves*, says a third, claiming that they represent all the choices we didn't make. Whatever they may be, for decades of sleep we've been frantic to tend to them, but lately, we've noticed a new desire to gather and harness them like pods of dolphins and let them pull us out of the knowable life.

*

When my friend Helen and her four sisters compare memories long after their father has died, it comes to light that all of them repeatedly sought refuge from his brutalities by the very same creek, though anticoincidentally, at different times; not even once throughout those years did the sisters ever encounter each other. This was in keeping with the stoicism with which each girl navigated childhood, though now, too late, they see that they could have turned themselves into a force, a tribe.

*

Are you on speaker? my friends and I ask each other irritably when our cell phone connections falter, but I always think of the kings and queens of antiquity; what wouldn't they have sacrificed to obtain the miracle of even this choppiest, most tentative of voice links—a portion of their gold, the lives of half their serfs, all their unmarried daughters?

*

Mentally combining all the sleep disorders of my friends, I'm blinded by a glorious archetypal pain goddess perpetually suspended in the shock of high-voltage wakefulness.

*

In fifth grade, my friends Barbara, Donna, and I dress up in thrift shop ball gowns many sizes too large for us and roller-skate around and around on her basement's cement floor to Monkees music while we argue about which Monkee is the cutest (though secretly, of course, we all know it's Davy Jones). In our minds, The Monkees themselves behold our puffy, shiny dresses and swift, wheeled strides with an intensity like Rhett Butler's when he gazes at Scarlett O'Hara on the big screen, since each of us *is* Scarlett, and Davy Jones is each of our only love as he croons that he's *counting on you*, but to us this is no anachronism because it's all one thing, one feeling that separates us from our younger sisters, who are still climbing trees and crawling through storm drains with the younger boys, entirely uninterested in what we're doing, though we not only lock the basement door but drag the ancient, decaying sofa over to bar it against them for good measure.

*

All my friends measure their mortal days by food and its transformations.

There are foods that contract with cooking and foods that expand, foods that stay the same size but change color, shape or consistency, and foods that remain inert.

There are foods that soak up water, broth, air, and juice, and foods that exude them.

There are foods we mince, chop, or pulverize, and foods that would break us if given half a chance—the popcorn kernel that takes out a filling, the spindly chicken bone that constricts the throat.

But everyone is eventually eaten by other eaters—earth, fire, water, the processes of decomposition, by time.

And what eats time?

Only time, of course, ravenous and self-consuming.

*

Crossings

At the Asylum for Foundling Mothers, candles blaze lavishly, wastefully in the windows all night long, but during the day we can glimpse no movement within, as though the residents have been rendered insensible after hours of excess.

We whisper about them during our ladies' teas and luncheons, each speculation passed along as gospel. They lounge around naked because their skin burns so hot with shame that it melts every kind of fabric; or they're covered from head to toe in the furs of fox kits, wolf and bear cubs, and even puppies and kittens, since stroking such softness is all that can quasi-soothe them. They never eat, battening on their own grief, or they gorge continuously on the Cake of One Hundred Eggs, plying the finest of needles to drill holes so infinitesimal that even after suctioning, each egg appears pure, inviolate, and then they bear the eggs through their secret passageway to the river to send them floating away in memory of their offspring, who abandoned them on the doorstep.

We dream about setting fire to that enormous edifice with paraffin-soaked rags, though it's not exactly that we want to kill the foundling mothers, we just want to smoke them out so they can take their suffering elsewhere, subsist as nomads—surely walking would be good for them, medicinal, even!

Nevertheless, it behooves us to prepare offerings to leave on their threshold: vials of our own breast milk, our little ones' baby teeth and hair clippings, and baskets containing their live kittens and puppies (which we claim have been sent to live on a farm). Our endeavors serve, we hope, to deflect disaster from our homes, ward off that dire change that can strike the inhabitants of any nursery or playroom without warning, for only our children's continued largesse allows us to abide on our own side of the street instead of behind those massive double doors.

If we approached in daylight, we'd have to dodge horses, vendors' carts, carriage wheels, and foot traffic, but it's midnight when we slip from our honorable feather beds to meet on the curb in our white nightgowns that glow in the lamplight as though to illumine our journey across the street, which, though brief, feels more like fording a flood than merely stepping on pavement. Then, after dropping our baskets with their wiggling, squirming inhabitants bound in cloths with the other propitiatory objects, we flee, holding hands as though the asylum has the power to suck in any lingerer.

Upon our return, we comfort each other with long, trembling embraces even though we suspect that more than a few of our basket-bearing, egg-cracking, child-minding sisterhood walk among us in disguise, hiding the persecutory powers that come with their true identities as changeling mothers.

Ledger

One significant birthday, you decide to record the names of everyone you've ever met.

Frequently, a name's escaped you so you've offered only a trailing *hello* or a telltale HEY THERE!, but now all day long they appear in your thoughts like strings of bubbles rising, especially when you're not free to write them down.

The names of your closest cousins. The name of your first best friend. The names, complete or in part, of the pet-store shopkeeper who sold you frozen infant mice to feel your corn snake; a string of babysitters (the one with the fat yellow braid; the one who taught you to whinny like a horse; the one who gave you pinkeye); the school bus driver, the hall monitor, your entire soccer team, including the alternates . . . and you still have decades to go! No matter how tangential the connection, each name is crisp and irreducible in its radiance of ordinary specificity, as though freshly minted from reality itself.

Meanwhile, you ponder the mathematics of convergence. You've heard that while the average villager of two hundred years ago would have encountered only the other people born there plus the rare passing traveler, *you'll* cross paths with about six thousand individuals over the course of your life. What happened to all the uninhabited name-space inside that theoretical villager—did it contract in a use-it-or-lose-it kind of way, or did the resonance of their neighbors expand to fill it?

And your own six thousand—does this number mark an outside limit, or will some denizen of a future hive city consider you just another primitive?

More to the point, how many more people will you meet for the first time?

You flip to the last page and begin inscribing each *new* name so that now you're working from both ends.

But when you write from the back, you use big letters to overflow the lines, since this is, you now see, an asymmetrical race toward the middle.

Elemental

Not long after texting surpassed cell phone and email conversations, we realized it wasn't the *content* of the messages that mattered, but only the small bright tone announcing one was still embedded in the social network.

What a relief! Now nobody had to waste time keying in actual words. Instead, empty bubbles proliferated, and people experienced pain relief as inflammation of the thumb's long-abused flexor muscle began to subside.

The logic of this change was soon applied to conversations as well. We jettisoned social rituals—remarks about the rain, inquiries about each other's well-being. And even beyond these niceties, the more we thought about it, the more unnecessary almost all our daily articulations had been. Why exhaust ourselves spinning out that conversational filigree when we could simply say "here," which in just one syllable covered the realms of discourse, negotiation, intrigue, rhetorical display, and verbal clutter by acknowledging existence itself?

Thus (except for in rare logistically complex situations), we intoned "here" back and forth to each other in pairs and clusters and groups all day long, and everything moved along so smoothly that soon even that one word was deemed excessive, replaced with a simple, fluid hand gesture. The city filled up with silence except for in the "talk" zones designated for education and child-rearing, where the young toiled at their studies in hopes of an early graduation into adult muteness.

Advertisers hired actors to merely point to their products on TV. Radios broadcasted a velvety spreading hush. Even politicians refrained from oration—in town halls and rotary club meetings, they performed the gesture, their audiences did the same, and then the aides rolled out the refreshment trays, a blessedly early evening for all. And consider the class reunion—didn't everyone already know that destinies rise and plummet, slide and skid in ambiguous lateral motion? Because the details are always more or less interchangeable, there was no need to recount them; how much more gratifying the choreography of hands and the feast of faces. For this scenario, full attendance was guaranteed.

In the absence of human babble, we began to notice sounds rising over the threshold of awareness so unobtrusively it was as though they'd always been there, which was, in fact, the case— all along, everything had been murmuring, whispering, lilting, sibilating, crooning, humming. Spoons chattered continuously in the dishwasher; behind the refrigerator door, eggs in their carton waxed loquacious; a steady flow of hissing colloquy rose from the stack of mail on the low glass side table in the hallway; in the backyard shed, shears emitted a quiet buzzing commentary; and in the yard, weeds and grasses together exuded an almost subsonic reverberation. Some of these sounds were pleasant to hear, others irritating or even painful. The saltshaker's speech tingled like tiny chimes and the garden hose gurgled melodiously, but the paper birch tree seemed to suffer from a raw, perpetually scratchy throat.

What could the world be *saying?* Frantic to know, we commissioned a crack team of technolinguists to create a multibillion-dollar omnitranslational device. Anticipation remained high during those decades of calculation and assembly; surely the result would prove to be nothing other than the secret of the universe, the answer to our most profound questions—who would expect less from the combined utterances of everything that had been constructed by our ingenuity and everything that had arisen so variously and spontaneously over time from the primal elements of creation?

At last, the day arrived. Holding our breath together, we watched on enormous public screens as the device finally ejected its printout displaying just one small word: the all-too-familiar "here."

Our collective disappointment was almost palpable. We'd so counted on everything to be ontologically different from ourselves! We'd so needed to be told something we hadn't already known! We'd craved—and paid for!—a revelation, but what had we gotten? Only old news.

Following disappointment came anger, swift and retaliatory. Some people growled and made threatening gestures toward the images of the translational device and the research team; others pointed to the borders, demanding a sentence of exile. But most experienced a sudden aversion to, and distrust of, the ritual hand gesture and the word it signified. What was "here," anyway? What did it even mean?

In families, in neighborhoods, in towns, cities and outlying farms, people spontaneously began to dismantle that word, breaking it open to see what was inside. And lo and behold, there was the entire language, crushed and massively compacted. After an awkward period of airing, untangling, and sorting, it turned out to be still usable despite our initial shyness as we filled our mouths with actual words and sent them out into the air: *Happy to meet you*, *How about this weather*, *Have a great day*, and then phrases and sentences of increasing length and complexity. From the depths of our kitchen drawers and the far reaches of our closet shelves, we unearthed our cell phones, which soon lit up with imperatives, conjunctions, interjections, gerund and participial clauses, and so on, even the hesitation forms like *uh* and *um* and *er*, which we now cherish like star rubies and cultured pearls.

Pockets

The old man sidles up to her bench in Central Park.

She's drinking her latte and listening, with equal parts frustration and fascination, to yet another podcast about how everyone has some kind of Great Work to accomplish.

She looks up at him cautiously. "May I help you?"

"I'm offering you the opportunity of a lifetime," he says, "but I have to whisper it."

The sooner she hears him out and tells him she's not interested, the quicker he'll leave, so, though having a stranger's breath in her ear is far from appealing, she nods, pauses the digital voice, and leans toward him.

He bends down close, cupping his hands around his mouth. "I'm here to transfer possession of the park to you," he says, "the real one, not this simulation we're in."

"What?" She pulls back and scoots away.

"Yes, it's folded into my coat pocket, clean and even at every corner, like origami."

"You're saying we're not in Central Park right this moment?"

Now she's whispering, too.

"Of course not," he says. "This is just a projection."

She scoots back a little further and begins to edge sideways for a quick getaway.

.

"No, it's true—since 1926, the actual, verifiable park has been the victim of thefts and counterthefts by the mobs and henchmen of the *New York Post* and the *New Yorker*. Sometimes one side had it, sometimes the other, and then there was that long, terrible period when the park itself was torn—the *New Yorker* took a third and the *Post* got the rest. Look around—do you see the seam where the workers did the repairs?"

She surveys the scene. Hot dog vendors, balloon sellers, dogs and their walkers, shrubbery, paths.

"No seam," she reports.

"Precisely! A dead giveaway. If we were standing in the *genuine* park right now, it would be obvious, running right over there across from the zoo. The seam is just one of eleven authenticity indicators."

Pondering the two institutions, as well as the nature of the city itself, she finds this scenario credible.

"So," she asks, "which side are you on?"

"Neither. I can't divulge how the park came into my possession, but it's time to pass it on to someone who can keep it safe from the media wars."

She wonders: Does she want to risk receiving stolen goods? If so, will she have to live on the lam with the black-ops details of two major journalistic enterprises forever on her tail? She hasn't even agreed to receive the contraband, yet she can feel her internal diction slipping to the level of old pulp magazine slang.

"Why me?" she stalls.

"Your outfit, of course," he says.

She doesn't have to look down to remind herself of what she's wearing, since it's always the same thing, which she washes out in the sink with Dreft every night before bedtime and drapes over the shower curtain rod to drip-dry.

It is the dress of many pockets: zippered pockets, sawtooth pockets, flap pockets, and patch pockets, as well as hidden and camouflaged pockets of various shapes and sizes, and pockets sewn into the lining against her skin.

This kind of dress runs in her family. Her mother, too, wore one every day, quite flashy since she had a thing for fat faux-pearl buttons; in each of her pockets languished an ancient, light-starved emergency dollar. Her grandmother's pockets were packed with Iowa loam so that whenever she felt homesick, she could pinch a bit out to savor its taste on her tongue.

Oh, those serene lamplit evenings, their kitchen table a cross between a sewing circle and a surgical theater, as all three of them sat together to microsuture worn spots.

Yet every morning they'd wake up to surprising configurations, since these pockets have personal itineraries of their own, migrating around a dress at will so you can never get a fix on them.

As for her own pockets, she's always left them empty to honor the idea of keeping possibilities open.

She sets down her latte and sighs. Yes, she thinks; her dress would indeed serve as a perfect refuge for the poor, beleaguered park, so apparently, this guardianship is not only her civic duty but her Great Work as well.

"All right," she says, "I'll do it," as she holds out her hand, expecting him to reach into his coat to begin the transfer. Instead, he gives a deep, formal bow, turns abruptly, and strides off.

Immediately she concludes that not only was he deluded, but that during the few moments she believed his story, she must have been deluded, too, for as every city dweller knows, this kind of thing is contagious. Still, as she stands to leave, she can tell that something is different: she's almost discernibly off-balance, like a ship listing slightly starboard.

Patting the pockets on her right side, she feels something so new and small that only an emptiness connoisseur would be able to detect it, no doubt deposited there by sleight of hand, the exact opposite of the pickpocket's maneuver. Only now does she understand her real motivation: not duty, after all, or even the allure of a Great Work, but a longing to hold the little packet in her palm, turn back its perfect folds, feel that slight weight increasing until it's so heavy she has to set it down as it expands around her.

Might this be the true Central Park of the heart, where the hands of the Delacorte Clock point always to midnight, and wolves hunt in packs through the trees?

Shore Patrol

Nobody ever drowned on my watch, though there were many who rose up spewing foam, faces we'd never seen before, illiterates all; we learned to our consternation, as though the shock of surfacing had displaced whatever education they'd acquired in their underwater world.

So I taught them the alphabet rhyme, which they dutifully recited in an accent we couldn't place, each of their voices struggling to make their way out as through a mouthful of clear glass marbles, but when we bade them part their lips so we could check for impediments, we found nothing but the multitudinous absence of the sea.

Gravity Pajamas

After so much suffering, all those failed attempts at a cure, the only treatment for the global insomnia pandemic turned out to be direct skin contact with jewels and precious stones. Now, thanks to the collaboration of geologists and fashion engineers, everyone can recover in sleepwear woven from microprocessed sapphires, emeralds, rubies, garnets, pearls, those little luminosities extracted from the earth and her waters.

The shaped, made-to-measure garment (far too heavy to lift, as though its fibers strain to return to the lithosphere) is wheeled into your bedroom on a dolly, then deposited by a crane-like device onto your massively fortified bed. At the end of the day, you maneuver yourself awkwardly into its opening; when the alarm rings, or in the night hours when you need to respond to the demands of passion, your bladder, or a restless baby, you work your way out of that mineral carapace, and leave it glittering on the sheets.

Though this is inconvenient, it's certainly preferable to the trauma of collective wakefulness, which was so terrible that people don't speak of it except on rare occasions, and even then, only by euphemism and indirection.

Nor do they talk about their sleep, commenting on its quality or recounting dreams; a new diffidence prevails, like the shyness of lovers reunited after an epic absence, as the one who stayed behind, noticing subtle changes in the other, wonders if this is indeed the longed-for union, or perhaps something else entirely.

Handiwork

It didn't take long for word to spread; in the night, someone had broken into the Thompsons' pasture and sliced off the tails of their horses. Only the stubs remained, clean as a chic French bob. The whole town was *sick about it, just sick! It's barbaric, it's an outrage, those tails will take years to grow back!*

According to some, however, it was partly the Thompsons' fault for not having invested in security cameras and guard dogs, though others maintained that cameras can be smashed and dogs silenced with drugged meat; with the recent influx of outsiders hungry for cheap land, no one could be safe anymore, no matter what precautions they might take.

A few murmured that the incident smacked of witchcraft: charm bags, divination, medicinal spells, and sex rituals they'd heard about but wouldn't sully themselves by describing. This was, of course, far-fetched, but even the skeptics were skittish; in town, people tended to edge away from each other instead of hanging around to chat. *What if it was one of our own?* everybody wondered but did not say.

They all wished the horses had *kicked those trespassers in the heads, kicked their heads right off.* Like the refrain of a local anthem, that phrase reverberated through homes and shops.

The horses themselves were uneasy, sweating and grinding their teeth; the stranger's scent still lingered in their velvety, flared nostrils, and now they had nothing to swish at the flies that were even thicker and more persistent than usual.

The young girls of the town felt unsettled as well; they too perspired and ground their small, human teeth, grieving for the horses' lost princess hair. This wasn't a normal summer. Their skin felt tight, prickly; the days and nights were so hot that no one splashed in the lake anymore because it would have been like swimming through soup; and their older sisters, who'd abandoned them for illicit moonlight car rides with boys, were too sleep drunk in the mornings to get up for their chores, so the little sisters had to resentfully cover for them.

That's why at the exact same predawn moment in their separate houses as they gazed at the older girls slumbering face down in their pillows with their hair spread out around them, they all had the same idea. They ran softly to their families' separate kitchens and workrooms and garages, reaching for the baling twine and shears. Their sisters were so deep in their dreams that they didn't even stir as the blades brushed the back of their necks.

The sun hadn't cleared the horizon when the little girls converged on the Thompson farm; no one saw them arrive, watched them work, or witnessed their departure. But everyone within hearing range would always remember the sound of Mary Thompson shrieking as she entered the pasture and saw the horses' long flowing tails.

Collectibles

When Carlie sees her mother waiting for her on the porch, arms crossed and thunder on her face, she knows she should have taken the long way around to the abandoned garden shed or at least paused at the edge of the woods to scope things out. Now it's too late—she's already in the open space of the yard with her sack, its inhabitant visibly vibrating within.

"Carlie! You release that ET this very moment! It needs to return to its flock."

"But I need it for my collection—I'd be the only kid with a live one! Besides, it's just a baby. It would hardly take up any space at all."

"That's not the point, Carlie. You know perfectly well that capturing them alive is illegal—it's been a hard enough year with the storms and the fires; do you want to be responsible for putting the whole family under an interdiction?"

Carlie sighs and shakes her head. "No, ma'am."

"Just be satisfied with the petrified ones you've found. Let it go—now! It might be scared in there. It might be suffering."

"Aunt Donna says they can't feel anything."

"Aunt Donna doesn't know; nobody does. Open up that sack before I come down there and make you do it."

As slowly as she possibly can without the appearance of disrespect, Carlie lowers the sack to the ground as if to do as she's told, then looks up at her mother, stalling.

"What does ET stand for, anyway? All the kids say it's for 'extraterrestrial,' but Alba said her dad told her it's something else that she couldn't remember."

"Well, it's nice to see you exhibiting a bit of curiosity instead of greed. I'll tell you about it when you do as I say."

There's a rustling sound; as the ET pokes its head up through the opening and fixes its red eyes on Carlie's mother, Carlie presses her advantage. "See, it's OK. It's just curious, it's looking around! Can't I at least hold it while you tell me? I promise I'll let it out right after."

Her mother frowns, then sighs. "All right, just for a few minutes, but be careful—it's not like they can be tamed."

Carlie ensconces herself on the porch swing, the sack on her lap as she almost but not quite leans against her mother. Swiveling its head from side to side as though assessing the situation with its fierce gaze, the ET emits intermittent squawks, but when Carlie gingerly strokes its scaly, spiny legs through the coarse material, it seems to relax a little.

"These creatures have been flying around in their strange geometric patterns for almost thirty years now," says her mother. "And 'ET' stands for 'extrusive thought.'"

"What does that mean?"

"'Extrusive' means 'coming out of,' so extrusive thoughts are free in the world instead of inside people's heads, where they used to circle around and around back when they were called 'intrusive thoughts.'"

Carlie ponders the spiky, knobby-skulled creature with its hoglike snout and whiptail. "I wouldn't want that in my head. It would hurt!"

"They didn't have these forms then; they expanded and solidified in the open air. When they lived inside people, they didn't cause physical pain, but their presence was still very disturbing. Sometimes they made their hosts so afraid or confused that they'd do terrible things to themselves or to each other, and sometimes they just made them worry they'd do those things, like my Uncle Bob—for most of his life, he had to live in a hospital, but when the Shift happened and the ETs flew out into the world, he was finally able to stay on his own."

"How did the ETs get free?"

"It happened all of a sudden when the earth's magnetic poles triple reversed themselves."

Carlie shivers. "What if the poles switch again? Could the ETs go back in?"

Her mother shakes her head. "The scientists who study them say that they and their offspring will always go through their life cycles on the outside now. In fact, the generation that's alive today has never even lived inside anyone's mind—one theory is that they're happier this way because their species didn't like buzzing around in people's brains any more than the people liked having them. Of course, there are all the new mental afflictions like thermal mutism and the dry stupors, but those have nothing to do with the ETs."

Carlie's mother sighs at the thought of everything she isn't saying. Carlie's too young to be told about the post-Shift attacks. Even now, it's painful to remember the heaps of bludgeoned ETs on the ground and the trapped ones beating their wings bloody against the walls of their containers, before anti-ET violence was outlawed when it became apparent that harm to the creatures caused their former hosts to suffer memory gaps and cognitive lapses.

Even with this expurgated history, something is bothering Carlie. "But how did they get inside people in the first place?"

"No one really understands how the mind works or where thoughts come from—do you?"

Carlie scowls skeptically, squinches her eyes shut and directs her attention within, expecting to find a clear organizing principle with which she can refute her mother, one of her favorite things to do. At first, she perceives the familiar items that make her Carlie— her secret plan to swim across the lake alone by the end of next summer or maybe the summer after that; her shame at still needing the comforting green glow of her triceratops night-light; fractions like tiny ants scuttling across the white field of a worksheet; the sensation of running her fingers over the ridges and indentations of her father's globe, which she's not supposed to touch. But then she becomes aware that some of her thoughts are overlapping, some are dissolving as she watches, and between others, there are blank floating spaces that seem to be made of nothing even as they constantly change shapes. Beneath all of this, there are last night's dreams, murky and inaccessible except as fragmentary images—herself in her sister's much-coveted red rain boots climbing a ladder that was leaning up against a cake as tall as her school building; a bathtub slipping over a waterfall's edge; her puppy, Acorn, struggling in a giant spider web, or had Acorn become very small?

Abruptly, she opens her eyes and pushes off from her mother, from the swing, rushes down the porch steps to the yard, and yanks open the sack.

There's a pause; then the fabric ripples violently as the ET bursts out in a startlement of quills and wings. It hovers for a moment as though orienting itself, then takes off in a southwesterly direction, uttering its characteristic guttural screech.

Dig

When we look back on that time, we remember how strange it was at first to see our children's sleds strung up on hooks, how disorienting it felt walking through dry streets, dry grass, dry forests that should have been glittering with heavy ice so we'd have had to constantly warn each other not to walk under those boughs— *You'd be taking your life in your hands!*—and then we all would have ventured out anyway, our brains tingling at the uncanny music of branches creaking and crackling in starlight.

We knew winter must have gone somewhere, since anything that enormous, that cruelly beautiful, doesn't just disappear, but though everyone speculated about it, by Christmas there was nothing left to say. The young people especially were at a loss; under normal circumstances they would have spent their free time careening down snowy hills, but now what were they to do?

In the second week of January, some middle schoolers tried to burn down an old outhouse on one of the abandoned properties just beyond town, then came running home, blabbing what they'd seen. Immediately, the dads marched off with axes and shovels.

Of course, they found the outhouse itself barely even charred, since it's not till tenth or eleventh grade that kids tend to attain arson competence, the crowning transformation of puberty. The ancient wooden toilet, which had long since been rocked off its setting, lay staved in and crumbling on the dirt floor.

Gathered around that ragged hole, the dads could see all the way down to the city of the dead, its spires and watchtowers with their high-mounted handless clocks, its public squares and sunken spring-fed pools, its albino horses pulling carts through the winding streets lit with gas lamps, and our ancestors shuffling along inside their veils of silence, never looking up.

The sight of the city wasn't new to the dads; in fact, we were all used to these portals popping open here and there as they found opportunity, and the sealing-over ritual had become so streamlined over time that it would have taken only a few minutes. By then, the sacrifice was no longer human or even animal, which was why each dad had an onion, a radish, a carrot, or a potato tucked in his pocket, root vegetables befitting the occasion. Immediately afterward, the dads would have gone for their celebratory rounds of beer. But now they stood there agape, stunned by the bright snow covering the underworld's rooftops and drifting in its streets, the glare of the icicles hanging from its eaves and gutters. Winter had abandoned us to bury itself alive.

And that's why our town has so many new holes, created to give everyone a bit of access. From spring through fall the municipal workers keep them capped with bulky metal covers, but every day between October's end and mid-March you can see people leaning over the edges for a flash of white or a whiff of chill to refresh us while we're still topside.

Cake-Heart
(a fable)

What a shock awaited the bakers' apprentices when they arrived at the post office early one morning balancing high stacks of cake boxes in their arms as usual.

There on the front steps stood the postmaster, frowning. "I regret to inform you," he announced, though he didn't appear regretful in the least, "that the postal service will no longer process, transport, or deliver packages containing baked goods of any kind."

The apprentices stared at him. They'd been trained for many kinds of disasters—kitchen fires, cakes that fail to rise, fallen cakes and cakes with sinkholes in the center, cakes that stick to the pans, deficiencies or excesses of shortening and sugar, temperamental ovens, overbaking, and exploding batter—but not for anything like this!

"We are the bakers' village," protested the chief apprentice as boldly as he could for one who was almost but not quite grown-up. "The entire realm relies on us!"

"Not my concern," replied the postmaster. "All that delicate handling was slowing down our services; our experts have determined that this change will allow the mail to move 27.3 percent faster." And he went back into the post office and shut the door.

Though the apprentices were horrified at the thought of everyone gathered for birthday parties, weddings, graduations, holidays, and family reunions, all cakeless, bleak, and inconsolable, there was nothing to do but report to their superiors. So back to the kitchens they trudged, murmuring anxiously about the fate of their intended careers, the survival of the village, and the well-being of the kingdom itself. Seeing the apprentices returning in such an agitated state, still balancing their stacks of boxes, though rather more precariously than before, the bakers knew that something was amiss, so they rushed to catch the cakes and hear the dreadful news.

Throughout that day and night, they all pondered together in the largest kitchen. If the realm were configured differently, some other method of cake deployment could be established—rotating teams of civilian bicycle couriers from the bakers' village, for instance, or a reverse setup in which emissaries from the other parts of the realm would travel to *them* to pick up their desserts, but because of the great distances between villages, and all the mountain ranges and large bodies of water in the way, without access to the postal service dirigibles, the situation was dire indeed.

As dawn was breaking, the chief baker announced, "The only solution is a drastic one. We must release the cakes to fly on their own."

"Release the cakes?! Preposterous! Inconceivable!" some of the bakers cried, for there would be high winds; there would be driving rain, snow, and ice, weighing the voyagers down; there would be flocks of marauding birds, and hungry sky pirates eager to hunt them down. With so many terrible fates a cake could suffer in the wild, wouldn't it be cruel, even criminal, to subject the cakes to such dangers? And even supposing none of these terrible things occurred, who would welcome an exhausted, traumatized dessert? Others, however, clamored their agreement with the chief baker.

Hubbub ensued, so they decided to put the matter to a vote. Everyone was murmuring to each other as they prepared to turn in their ballots, when all of a sudden the head baker said sharply, "Stop! Be quiet! Listen!" In the stillness, they could barely hear a gentle thumping from the stacked boxes. It was the cakes themselves, rising slightly to bump against the inner lids, for they'd been awake the whole time, considering the situation, though usually they slept until their boxes were opened (sometimes if you were very slow and careful, you could catch them changing colors as they dreamed).

"The cakes have made their wishes known!" cried the youngest apprentice, forgetting his lowly station. "They're telling us to set them free!" And indeed, this was so evident that not even the naysayers could deny it.

So it was that by the time the sun had risen above the horizon, the cakes were all lined up outside the kitchens in their individual boxes. There were tall cakes and short, squat cakes; fat, heavy cakes and cakes of all froth and foam; finicky, fastidious cakes with the souls of purebred poodles—high-strung, confectionary marvels prone to shivering with agitation at the slightest upset. Planted in the frosting of each rounded crown was a small paper flag with the handwritten address of the cake's destination.

The apprentices raised the lids and stepped back. The very air seemed to shimmer with anticipation as the cakes began to ascend. The angel food cakes struggled a bit with initial liftoff but managed just fine as they attained altitude. The fruitcakes rose straight up like corks from bottles, and then plowed steadily along horizontally like sturdy little tugboats. Once all the cakes had cleared the level of the rooftops, some sliced through the sky with the elegance of silver swans; some moved in a sequence of bursts punctuated by brief, hovering pauses as though hopping on nothing at all; some floated languidly on prevailing breezes; some proceeded with balletic leaps and turns; and some moved together like flocks or confectionary armadas, though most soared solo. Surprisingly, the denser the cake, the more swoops and loops it performed.

A small number would arrive at their destinations in a few hours, but many would have to navigate great distances by starlight. All knew instinctively that they must strive to travel above cloud level, to work with, not against the winds, and to position themselves directly beneath the high-flying pirate ships, almost but not quite attaching themselves like puffy barnacles so the pirates would never even glimpse them.

As the weeks went by, messages came back one by one to the bakers' village. Each of these voyagers had arrived safe and fresh and sleek, invigorated by their exertions as though the flight had plumped them up, refreshed them!

And that's how this realm became famous for its self-propelled traveling cakes. The bakers were so relieved and happy that they became playful as they worked and began baking in all sorts of treasures: rings, coins, puzzles, small ceramic dolls with even smaller dolls nested within. Customers everywhere were delighted; many ordered cakes with personal messages rolled up in scrolls inside— love notes and marriage proposals and congratulatory wishes, some in codes, ciphers, or musical riddles—it made everyone grin to think about all those surprises flying through the air.

Of course, over the years, not every cake arrived as planned. A few proved to be poor navigators, or fell apart midair, or were blown off course to eventually plunge into the ocean. Now and then a cake absconded and was never seen again, its death lonely and unmarked. There were cakes that started out sweet and ended up bitter. There were cakes that arrived so damaged that they were almost unrecognizable. A family out for their evening stroll observed but was not able to rescue one cake completely furred over with the bees that were bearing it away. There were even rumors of cake hauntings, which consisted of missing cakes and inexplicable, pervasive fragrances.

The bakers were such devoted artisans that every time they learned of a cake's demise, they gave it a full funeral in absentia, with a large smooth round stone standing in for it in the coffin of its own original box. But such was the cakes' general prowess that the little cemetery remained permanently underpopulated. The intrepid, heroic nature of the average cake was now so universally admired that of all possible compliments one could ever hope to receive, the highest would be forever "cake-heart."

The Quest

You can tell Orpheus has passed through your neighborhood by the wreckage in his wake: churned earth where trees uprooted themselves to follow, debris of buildings that dragged themselves after him, vulnerable to the violence of his music—also the motley collection of everyone within earshot plus the families, friends, and neighbors they've summoned by text: VERIFIED SIGHTING ON ARMSTRONG AVENUE JUST PAST CVS HEADING SOUTH. Each time, everyone drops what they're doing and rushes to bask in those tones *like a geyser of molten diamonds*, they say, or *a surge of cresting light*.

Blah blah blah, thinks Orpheus, who finds that hyper-Romantic imagery distasteful, and despises the music he can't help emitting even in his sleep. That's why he labors to make his voice louder with every step, as though he could heave out the sound to lift, fly briefly, then sink from its own weight, clogging the mouths of rivers, splitting asphalt, crushing houses and their inhabitants, asphyxiating the entire human race, he wouldn't care so long as he was free of it. He no longer seeks that barely recognizable wraith languishing on the bridal throne in Hades under miles and miles of rock—what he craves is tantalizingly near, though inaccessible, smothered by ream upon ream of melody like heavy gold brocade: the silence within him before he began to sing.

Going Under

We sleep when our skin becomes saturated with night; we sleep to escape from noonday glare-flat light, ghost light, the hour when spirits walk, as the ancients believed. We sleep because we're exhausted by the seventy-one dimensions of sky bearing down on us, inexorable as stone. We sleep because we've run out of thoughts or we have too many thoughts or the spaces between the thoughts have grown thick with a soft gray substance that's neither fur nor mold but like them in texture, exuding a subtle soporific fog. Some of us sleep as punishment, sent supperless to our severe and narrow beds. Others sleep for indulgence, arms outflung, luxurious expanse unfurling. We sleep incidentally, we sleep incrementally. We sleep exuding dreams like the voluptuous ink clouds of an octopus garden. We sleep on our feet like horses; curled over the steering wheels of parked cars; and sometimes, terrifyingly, as we drive. We dote on sleep as if it's a delicate only child that we'd ply with bonbons, bedeck with pearls, and daub with tinctures of crushed diamonds plucked from the coronation tiaras of popes and queens. We bargain with sleep, we chastise it, we compete with each other over its supreme inadequacies—"I had the worst night!" "No, mine was far more wretched!" We stalk our sleep, dragging our paltry nets and snares behind us as we crawl over miles of crushed glass and barbed wire toward where it was last sighted. We sleep in layers; we sleep in stages; we sleep through sequences of false awakenings as though tumbling down the stairs of sleep through subbasement after subbasement in interminable descent. We sleep through the first, second, third, and fourth watches of the night and in the intervals between them that are made not of minutes but of slippage and unlikeness. We could say that sleep is a waste of time if we knew what time is. We could say that time is a waste of sleep, but while dreaming, we're everyone we've ever been, and we're the death-self we like to pretend is a stranger though it's been our nearest companion from the very first breath. We sleep incandescently; we sleep phosphorescently. In sleep, the body breathes as houses do, no matter how many layers of caulk and sealant the owners apply, slow seepage of breath, voices, memories, aromas, and soulglow. Who lived in your house before you, what dream residue brushes your face like spider silk as you cross the threshold between rooms? And long before there were houses, the land itself slept during great freezes when the fish dreamt in suspension, torpid under layers of ice, and during the aftermaths of floods when everything was tranced and still. That was the sleep of history before the twinkle of electronic devices in every room like domestic constellations. Now sleep texting is on the rise, since everyone beds down near or even with their phones as though connected by an unseen umbilical cord, so in the morning, pixels reveal the heart's occult detritus like broken shells and fish bones exposed by a receding tide: complaints, declamations, confessions, personal manifestos, breakups, propositions and proposals—yes, the culture of sleep is changing—there's sleep shopping, too, a retail extravaganza in the emporium of night. And that's only the beginning; soon, all vehicles will be autonomous, sentient metal pods bearing slumberers chipping away at their sleep debt's compound interest so that dreaming will be associated with motion itself and the very act of getting into a vehicle will cause us to nod off—we'll wake up just in time to stumble into work, though there's something about sleep that will never be commodified, never turned into capital because the real reason we sleep is for relief from the sensation of being always, repeatedly, and continually ourselves, ourselves when we wake up in the morning, ourselves when the clock strikes midnight, and in between, as we pause to check during micromoments of awareness during the day, still ourselves—who would have thought it?

The Last Space-Bearer

And now the entire family was gathering around the child as she pulled herself up to stand, then overbalanced and fell, landing plushly on her diapered rump. "Ah," they exclaimed, "she's begun her getting-ready-to-walk story."

Soon she would move through her drinking-from-a-cup story and her singing-the-alphabet story, then later, all the various components of the education, vocation, and civic responsibility stories, etc., for this city's primary axiom was that the world contained a fixed number of predictable recurring stories.

In every generation, however, there was always one individual, chosen by lot, who dedicated their adult life to becoming as story-free as possible. On their twenty-first birthday, this person, known thereafter as the space-bearer, bade farewell to their family and friends, then retreated to a solitary mountain cabin to do nothing for the rest of their days, a vocation more indispensable than that of the doctor, the police chief, or even the trash collector, for without the stabilizing effect of this storyless space, who knew what kind of chaos might ensue? To spare their space-bearer even the food-gathering story and the small-talk story, valley dwellers regularly left baskets of fruit and cheese on the cabin doorstep in the dead of night. Each new space-bearer hosted more emptiness than the one before, receiving in a single long exhalation of dying breath the aged officeholder's space as well as that of all their predecessors, though nobody knew whether death made this release possible or the release itself was fatal.

And so things went, century after century, until that fateful day when from a distant university came tidings of an astonishing discovery based on innovative gravitational algorithms: the whole world was teeming with stories that could not be perceived because they were too immense and particulate, or too infinitesimal and compact, or oscillated too swiftly between subliminal and supraliminal frequencies.

Had they always been present, or were they just now flooding in through some dimensional rip or tear? Or perhaps there had been only a few at first, but they'd proliferated, attaining critical mass. Everywhere else, people regarded this situation with indifference if they thought about it at all, but here citizens flinched and ducked through their days as though they could sense these unseen stories pressing in around them. Soon no one would have room to move or even breathe! At night, the adults cried out from nightmares of being crushed by story avalanches, and the children, who accepted this behavior as no less arbitrary than any other aspect of the grown-up world, abandoned their little beds to try to sing their parents back to a more placid sleep.

In this crisis, of course, everyone's thoughts turned to the space-bearer, who could provide immediate relief. True, the act of emitting that reservoir of emptiness might prove fatal, but they would be sure to set up a statue as an appropriate part of the veneration-and-homage story, and once everything was safe again, they could send up a replacement to start over.

That's why one morning, the space-bearer found on their doorstep not the usual food basket but a committee of three dignitaries.

"Times have changed," said the lead dignitary. "The tradition no longer suffices. To save us from imminent annihilation by stories, we need you to release all the space inside you."

The space-bearer thought for a moment. "Are you sure that's what you want?" they asked each of the dignitaries, and each affirmed the decision.

"Very well," said the space-bearer, and stepping back a bit, they opened their mouth and exhaled, the oceanic expanse pouring out from between their lips to flow down the mountain in torrents that would make the most impressive waterfall in the world seem paltry by comparison.

Overwhelmed by that pressure and roaring, the dignitaries couldn't tell whether the process was taking hours or days, but at last the most ancient space of all from countless generations ago surged out in a gust so powerful that it lifted the space-bearer off the ground and swept them away.

For a while after that, the dignitaries stood rooted in place, unable to move at all. Then, blinking and stretching as though coming out of a trance, they finished off the leftover cheese and fruit and trudged down the mountain together.

Upon reentering the city, the first sight that they beheld was a set of three tall, green-tinged copper statues of themselves, their appearances significantly enhanced, with a plaque stating that they, the dignitaries, were presumed to have perished in the Great Upheaval a hundred years ago. This was how they discovered that their presence during the release of all that storyless space had reconfigured their relationship with time itself; the space-bearer and all their former fellow citizens now resided in the cemetery, and as they wandered the streets and ventured into public buildings everyone they met was a stranger with bizarre apparel and an unidentifiable accent.

Everyone agreed that the dignitaries' arrival from the past was remarkable, but what was to be done with them? They could no longer serve in their former roles, of course, since their understanding of the world was completely outdated. After much debate, it was decided that the best place for them would be fourth grade, where they could learn about the current social norms and the historic developments of the intervening years. Despite the dignity of their former office, they found it comforting to sit with the nine- and ten-year-olds, and even enjoyed the school lunches, as institutional cuisine had improved since their day.

Along with their classmates, they learned that when those enormous quantities of emptiness had flowed through the streets, supersaturating the atmosphere, everyone suddenly began lurching and staggering in slow motion as they felt their stories fly away from them, breaking apart. Mail piled up in mounds at the post office because the sorting and delivery story components had spun loose from each other. Apples rotted in their barrels because the apple-picking part of the harvesting story was no longer attached to the taking-to-market part. Lovers attempting to embrace found themselves walking right past each other, arms closing on air, for now there was so much space that everything occurred disconnectedly and in slow motion.

It was a vertiginous period indeed, but after a while, some of the space began to gradually dissipate, wafting out to sea, and some was dispersed with air cannons, and eventually, the painstaking work of recovery began despite lingering disorientation. Neighbors helped each other sort through the strewn and scattered story parts, though many didn't fit together as they had before—no doubt their shapes had been changed when they'd fused with free-floating bits of the invisible stories which must also have been blasted apart by the deluge.

The last space-bearer, who had landed on their stockinged feet in the city square with that final rush of breath, encouraged people to experiment with new configurations, incorporating holes and gaps to host the rest of the buoyant, wafting traces of emptiness. Soon the city was filled with wonder and surprise—a woman in full bridal regalia suddenly abandoned her own wedding procession to go trout fishing alone; a demolition crew interrupted their work to enjoy a game of hide-and-seek around the stairwells and porticoes of the condemned building; a meteorologist and a bookie worked together to take bets on the speed and trajectory of thunderheads. Everyone gave up on the idea of determining how many stories there could be.

Over the decades, the little cabin on the mountaintop fell into ruin, disintegrating so completely that no hiker or explorer would ever be able to guess that it had stood there sturdily for generations. And as for the dignitaries themselves, they so enjoyed being in fourth grade that permission was granted for them to remain there indefinitely, savoring seasoned fish sticks with ketchup in little fluted cups at the long lunch tables.

Universal Cognitive Maintenance

After its inception, everyone was both happier and more distracted.

Fear of forgetfulness, of the forgotten itself? Gone!

Gloom about the ephemeral nature of experience? Also gone.

On the other hand, now every citizen spent a lot of time rummaging through the labyrinthine stacks of Storage and Retrieval—no simple task, considering the chaos of each person's memories, sensations, and speculations.

Often, it would turn out that other forgotten thoughts seemed more desirable than the one the seeker wanted to locate, so it wasn't uncommon to trudge through the exit gate later and more laden down than one had anticipated.

Mental life became increasingly recursive, as people now felt that they could fully delve into their own life experience instead of scurrying over its surface like characters running across the top of a high-speed locomotive in an old movie.

As one commentator proclaimed, *We are at last endogenous to ourselves.*

Before long, a new psychiatric disorder became common: "anxiety when forced to spend time away from Storage and Retrieval."

Paid "S&R" leave was the first benefit people checked for with every employment package.

And so many people found it convenient to schedule meetings on the premises that Starbucks set up a network of locations throughout the facilities.

When it became popular to camp out among the stacks, instantly accessing each night's dreams each morning, a host of hotels and Airbnbs sprang up; these eventually gave way to houses, then villages, and finally, cities complete with business districts, suburbs, and gated communities.

The outer world has become increasingly depopulated, except for a few resisters. Some are uncomfortable about the very idea of an inner life, some cultivate a spirituality of impermanence, and some are simply too impatient to engage in all that sifting and sorting, but all enjoy the luxuries of the abandoned residences and shopping malls. And there's the little community in the old neighborhood that outsources their connection to their mental past. When one of them needs to retrieve a particular cognitive event, they send out a list of specifications to a day laborer who trudges to S&R to select a half dozen or so according to the target thought's general characteristics and hauls them back across the border to be examined. This occurs as many times as it takes; afterward, all the near-miss thoughts are returned only slightly worn from handling.

Most influential of all, however, are the racketeers working the shadow economy who engineer artificial cognitive data to be smuggled *into* storage by stealth operatives, often middle-management double-dippers. In the early years, these counterfeits were relatively simple—a mother wanted her daughter to cherish a few brighter images of sophomore year, for instance, or a district attorney needed several witnesses to discover a particular memory when called to the stand.

But as increasing numbers of consumers demanded synthetic recollections (some ordinary, some ecstatic or depraved, others ecstatic *and* depraved), these fictions became more elaborate.

Clusters of adult siblings purchased family-narrative do-overs going back generations. Various interest groups used their collective buying power to purchase what came to be known as "consensual histories," which themselves were subject to alteration as internal dissent arose. Of course, authentic memories that contradicted fresh fabricated ones had to be identified, isolated, and destroyed by the extractors, a network of stealth operatives with their own profiteering structure.

With all these layers of financial opportunity, no one was surprised when organized crime moved in. Now the mob and the police strive to thwart each other in a sequence of intimately choreographed maneuvers; after every successful raid, more thought labs pop up behind different fronts.

Most citizens look back on their pre-Cognitive Maintenance selves with a gratifying mixture of compassion and condescension—*of course* they were always misplacing all that mental content ranging from the previous night's dreams to great swaths of their childhoods! Nothing could be more forgettable than the artifacts of a fixed, immutable past languishing in a solitary brain.

Reverse Paper

It appears in your life suddenly and without warning from who knows where, all those thin, slick sheets that repel information and reflect nothing. One moment everything is as it's always been; the next, knee-deep reams of reverse paper flood your living room, cascade down your front steps, and inundate your office.

It can't be burned, cut, torn, or punctured, and you can't even throw it away, since immediately upon detecting that intention in your touch, it becomes too heavy to lift; you have to wade through it, find a way to function despite its presence.

But one day, a woman who'd suffered a backyard infestation plunked herself down in the middle of it and began turning the paper's edges, creating tiny, deft folds and pleats. When a few neighbors happened to see what she was doing, word got around, and after someone set up a webcam, it wasn't long before the whole world was watching her hands tuck and crease and double as she created a pup tent just big enough for one.

Then in she went while everyone held their breaths, emerging a few minutes later, apparently no worse for the wear. When asked about her experience, she stated that while she was inside, she'd been unable to hear her own thoughts, a sensation she described as disorienting though not exactly unpleasant. Though she declined to repeat the exploit, she'd put too many hours into creating the tent to want to take it down, so all kinds of people flocked there to wait days for their turn to enhance their meditation practice, rehearse being dead, or temporarily escape tormenting memories. Some speculated that they became invisible during their stay, a claim which could neither be proved nor refuted, like the condition of the proverbial refrigerator light.

Eventually, wanting to reclaim her privacy as well as give the trampled grass a chance to recover, she went out one midnight and started folding the paper backward. This had the effect of diminishing it until after hours of iterative creases, the whole mass of it was finally small enough to slide into a matchbox, at which point it spoke for the first and only time.

How am I going to breathe? it asked in a thin, silky whisper. *You will subsist on reverse air*, she said, and she was right.

Literary Contrivances of the Future

Not like the book wheels of previous centuries, those bulky vertical monstrosities with their double mirrors and epicyclic gears.

Not like the slightly more recent reading hats, whose migraine-inducing straps and bolts bit into flesh as the books revolved at a preset velocity according to a scholar's absorption capacity.

Such devices merely embodied the very limitations they were fashioned to overcome, since no matter how swiftly you cranked the haft or flicked your eyes back and forth, you could still proceed only page by page by page in a sequence of ones, your mind toggling between texts, starting over again and again as the apparatus repeatedly failed to fulfill that dream of eliding the gaps between volumes, that dream of all the words hitting the brain's pleasure centers instantaneously like the lights of a tiered city winking on together as the books rotate so swiftly they appear to be motionless while passersby erroneously exclaim, "Why does that reader caged inside a whole-body oaken crown gaze fixedly at just one page?"

Nor can any of the contemporary models serve as vehicles for transcendence, not even the portable panoramic-transmitter headset constructed of ultra-high-molecular-weight polyethylene, spider silk, aerogel, and silica nanofibers—which is why we have to hold out for injectable literature, entire libraries syringed into the cerebrospinal fluid of citizen after citizen as demand crashes the markets, bringing to a close the long, tragic era of mutually reinforcing capitalism and existential loneliness in one shared simultaneous internal read.

Gloves

All over the world the multitudinous tribe of gloves is unraveling. Firefighters are aghast, along with chefs, nail technicians, surgeons and their beleaguered assistants, the circus mistress and her troupe of clowns, even Mickey Mouse himself, small and protohuman at the cartoon piano as he gazes transfixed at his eight fingers popping out of their puffy white swathing. Cotton, leather, latex, silk, from heavy-opaque to sheer, all those tips splitting open like sea anemones blooming in time-lapse sequence as fibers loosen and fray down the length of the fingers toward the palm. With our hands we have done terrible things to the earth and to each other, and this is either our warning or the first phase of our punishment.

Recurrence

One day while you're on your morning walk, a flash of light catches your eye and you look up to see a window gleaming naked in the great elm's branches.

Of course, you can't help but sigh at the thought of yet another sky-house sailing through the night, slowing, hovering, giving up height just long enough to release the window into that leafy bower as though laying it down in a four-poster, then rising and gliding toward the coastline and out over the open water to deposit a sister window on the waves like a visual portal to the sea from above or to the clouds from underwater.

As it travels, the house will let go of doors and walls, joists and floorboards, until what passes overhead is merely the structure's memory, its ghost.

At the thought of this, you frown and shake your head. Yes, times are hard everywhere, no one disputes this, but these self-dismemberment rituals have to stop.

Monograph on a Giant Lullaby

Since their speech evolved from that of their rock forebears, interpretation is uncertain, riddled with gaps. Also, giant songs occur at such a low frequency that even specialized recording devices can capture only fragments.

Despite these obstacles, scholars have compiled rough translations of what appear to be variant versions of a single lullaby.

The cycle always begins with an acknowledgment of the child's restlessness: "Thunder on the mountain: young limbs thrash, eyes refuse [to close]" represents a typical opening.

This passage is usually the most elaborate of the sequence, as though the child enjoys hearing at length about its own powers of resistance.

The second stanza, which depicts the great lineage of giants dreaming in dens and caves throughout the world, includes multiple references to mountains so far beneath the surface that translators assumed them to be merely mythological until 2019, when seismologists announced the discovery of subterranean mountain ranges some four hundred miles deep.

The words "fold" and "twist" are repeated in most of the versions, evoking imagery of giants' recumbent frames embedded in rocks and boulders.

The third section is always a litany of mocking invectives against humans, portrayed as soft, dependent upon puny artificial shelters which the giants call "weak-walls" (or perhaps "fail-walls").

Though the extended passage never mentions giants themselves, it extols them through implied contrast, intensifying the child's kinship identification.

The depiction of humans' pitiable, self-protective nature functions as a transition to the fourth stanza's "Glory of Giants" theme, which exalts the eventual breakage and dispersal of their enormous body parts throughout the lithosphere by heat, ice, erosion, and compression.

Some scholars have speculated that this correlates with the many references to danger in human lullabies such as plague ("Ring around the Rosie") and cradles falling from trees ("Rock-a-Bye Baby"); as the poet Lorca remarked in his cross-cultural analysis, the motif of most lullabies is "Alone you are, alone you shall be."

However, the human mother's crooning melody undercuts that message so that her child can float off to sleep on the flow of this contradiction as she releases her anxieties through lyrically coded expressions.

Giant sonics, on the other hand, are made up of harsh raspings and gratings that can be produced only by their particular vocal apparatus, evoking images of enormous boulders ground violently against each other, assuring the young that they are not alone because they participate in the earth's movements.

These repeated images of dismemberment apparently quiet juvenile giants' natural agitation as they slip into happy dreams of their own severed limbs wedged into the shearings of discordant landscapes, their own fingers and toes starry outcroppings along distant moraines and glacial tills.

The fifth and final stanza praises the giant child's heart, the only part of the body that is materially distinct from the rest of its body—not solid, but a living ecosystem of pulpy, densely matted moss, lichen, and wood-decay fungi destined to break or be torn apart upon exposure, enriching the soil, which through centuries of pressure will become the rock flesh of future giants.

Clearly, their relationship with time is gratifying, not tragic. In fact, though their language contains no abstract nouns, their syntax suggests that they believe the destruction/dissemination of their bodies actually *causes* time, which they apparently view as a simultaneous rather than a sequential phenomenon.

For them, everything occurs at once: the dissolution of their limbs and organs; the lift and thrust of bedrock; the collapse of surface soil; the shifting of tectonic plates; the appearances and disappearances of mountains, sinkholes, land bridges, oceans; the fleeting flashes of plant and animal life.

Perhaps they experience time in this way because their life cycle is based on geologic, not sexual, processes, as larger, older giants take on kinship responsibilities for giants freshly emerging from rocky structures.

These findings have reshaped our understanding of their perpetual internecine conflicts; only now do we see that what we had mistaken for aggression is in fact the generative impulse—damage dealt is no different from damage received, which is no different from extrusions of new life.

Human flesh contains trace metals from ancient granite, so we too, though more distantly, evolved from rocks. Though giants are our far-flung cousins, they view us as an unwholesome recent species and eschew all association with us, even driving away any of their kind tainted with petroglyph marks; such outcasts form the fiercest of clans.

Nevertheless, perhaps our captive specimens of giant young (acquired at such a high cost to human reconnaissance teams) can sense that shared mineral prehistory.

We hope they find this consoling, along with the lullabies streamed through laboratory speakers while we probe and dissect, seeking to discover how consciousness can be fused with the inorganic so that those of us selected for survival can flee the cities, mind-leaping into basalt and obsidian as ice caps melt and fail-walls burn.

Forests

For most mothers the arboreal shift occurs gradually, filament by filament, leaf by leaf, so their families' shock seems disingenuous; if they'd been paying the kind of attention that domestic life tends to discourage, they might have noticed the oaky scent of a mother's breath as she leaned in for a goodnight kiss, they might have glimpsed traces of sphagnum in the shower drain coiling with strands of her hair (though only if they were the ones to regularly scour it, which is rarely the case).

Of course, each transformation is unique, and not all forests are female or even dendrological, though each dances by some form of branching or flowing, whether vertically, horizontally, or in place. The lexical mother, for instance, who belongs to the cloud-mother family, inhabits a variety of alphabets breathed out in word tendrils that rise to form the moving structures of the aerial wilderness above, from sparse cirri to lofty vertical towers and colossal back-building thunderheads. Now *that's* a forest indeed, albeit a falling one, ever returning to earth to continue the cycle.

But the mothers aren't uniformly benign. Yes, it's possible to not only enter the territory of the deciduous mother, known also as the oxygen-cathedral mother, but to rope yourself into its branches for the night, dreaming the kinds of dreams possible only in its embrace. If you feel you must venture into a rainforest mother, however, don't let its humidity and apparent torpor lull you into somnolence—the surplus of venomous organisms exceeds human taxonomic capacities, and at any moment, a python or boa constrictor might drop down upon you from the canopy. Despite such dangers, the fact that commercial interventions have rendered great swaths of the rainforest mother ragged and torn is neither anomalous nor to be celebrated, since the more resource-abundant the mother, the more endangered it's likely to be—take, for instance, the coral mother, who before our very eyes has become such a blanched and brittle ghost that tourists snap off its fingers and slip them into their pockets like they're pilfering the knucklebones of some local saint.

Though we've always understood the mothers' situation to be intermittently precarious, we reassured ourselves that these cycles must be natural; surely there was no cause for alarm. Only recently has the new spectroscopic equipment revealed that on the metaphysical level every mother is in fact a kinetic environment, which means it's possible to be at the same time a burning mother and a kelp mother or a mother of ice.

And not only that, but we also now know that their observable surface area represents only a small portion of their essence, the rest of which is made up of unseen rhizomatic emanations entangling us all. So how can we differentiate our sufferings from theirs as they murmur together in their imperceptible colloquy of flame?

The Day We Awoke to Find
All the Animals Gone

We agreed they'd been wise to leave us, though of course we felt forlorn without their chirps and chatterings, their snufflings, snorts, and purrs, the percussion of claws on linoleum, the solid feel of their bulk pressed up against us for food or affection, the slurp-slurp at bowl or trough, the rhythmic thump of vigorous scratching, the resonant rustle of wingbeats, so it's no wonder we fell into our collective frenzy of cherishing their artifacts (the collar, the dish, the leash, the saddle, the bridle, the currycomb, the fuzzy blanket, the still-indented pillow); it's no wonder we spent a whole year retrieving residual fur in clumps and strands by ripping open vacuum cleaner bags, scraping couch cushions, air filters and the beds of our pickup trucks. We wandered the world salvaging feathers, too, and fish and reptile scales translucent, easily torn.

After those long millennia together it should have been simple to re-create some semblances of their forms, but our species-specific memories were collapsing, so our hands stuttered in their work, and the glued-and-sutured creatures seemed unfamiliar, bizarre. They refused to make even the smallest sound, an extra layer of loss since by that time nobody could quite recall the cry of the turtlehawk bearing its heavy shell through the sky, or the voice of the dogkey braying as it dug with its claws and burrowed with its snout as though seeking to unearth some remnant of a once-thriving people interred by time along with their beasts and stories.

The Bees

We plant sage, speedwell, coneflower, aster, setting up waves of continuous bloom; we clear away mulch to accommodate ground nesters; we leave fallen branches and rotting logs undisturbed for their habitation; we place red bowls of water in dry places.

Wingless, lumbering, and tragically imprecise, we'll never be more than their servants, their fleshy megafauna, yet we rehearse their dances and mime their movements. On every street, you'll see a citizen standing atremble, straining to emit a high nasal hum, the closest we can come to our own version of hovering.

That they possess a collective soul was never the question, but whether in time we humans might evolve one.

Teleology

What have we been up to since it was announced that the sheer edge of time is approaching—or maybe *we're* moving toward *it*—do we panic in the streets, do we party, do we pray?

No, we're busy with the usual scouring, scrubbing, folding, sorting, stacking, slipping things into drawers and files, stuffing bags with paperwork for the shredder.

It's unclear why our species feels the need to accumulate so much stuff. William of Ockham admonished us to refrain from multiplying entities beyond necessity, but he too—or rather, his servants—devoted many hours a day to dusting and winding his hundred clocks, though ninety-nine of them could surely have been discarded.

Now here we are at the brink of cataclysm, still overwhelmed by not only our belongings but everything we need to contain them (file folders, envelopes, clips and binders, shoe trees, plastic tubs and bins, laundry hampers, shower caddies, clothes hangers, towel racks, bookends) and sanitize them (brooms, mops, wipes, swipes, steamers, sponges, brushes, detergents, degreasers, acids, abrasives).

And as we clean, we debate the possibility of achieving perfect order before the end.

The pessimists are certain it's impossible; quoting Camus (*We must imagine Sisyphus happy*), they labor only for the sake of the tasks themselves.

The optimists try to forecast what kind of margin we might anticipate, like that interval before guests arrive when everything's serene and shining, and you gaze with satisfaction at the vacuum cleaner's tracks along the carpet: an hour, fifteen minutes, a mere second or two?

But for our new prophets, the question is irrelevant; they preach that if we work hard enough, and with true enough intention, at the final moment, a miracle will occur: everything we've manufactured will vanish as the heavenly powers purify the entire world by editing out all the objects of employment, deployment, and manipulation—coffee cup, keyboard, spatula, scalpel, spade— solely to glorify the dance of hands in the world like birds swooping, plummeting, turning and rising to turn again, finger-flocks everywhere, unencumbered at last.

Distance at Very Close Range

What a scene! All through the streets, everyone was craning their necks to gaze up at the canopy that covered the city. For longer than anyone could remember, it had housed an intricate arrangement of embedded pulleys, ropes, and nets, but now, inexplicably, the entire apparatus was gone, leaving the fabric stark and bare.

This is how the system had worked: you'd be going about your ordinary tasks when suddenly a dream would come upon you and you'd begin to act it out, pummeling an unseen enemy, coupling with an invisible lover, cooking an imaginary meal, conducting your half of an otherwise inaudible argument. According to protocol, the nearest bystander would tug sharply on the nearest low-hanging rope, releasing a net to entangle and immobilize you. Everyone nearby would avert their eyes until the dream had run its course, then you'd self-extricate and give the rope a second tug to send the net back up till it was needed again at that location.

But without the nets, no one had any idea what might happen next. Would the government send soldiers to restrain dreamers, placing the entire society under martial law? Or worse, would everyone simply be left defenseless against their unconscious impulses? An informal height-and-girth-based buddy system sprang up as friends pledged to take turns restraining each other.

They were all still deep in conversation about this emergency when the mayor's messengers ran through the parks and market-places crying out: *Have there been any dreamers here?* And indeed, it was soon apparent that since the nets' disappearance, no one had experienced a single dream.

At this point the people found themselves on the verge of panic, because as everyone knows, dream deprivation brings break-down. If they'd been threatened by an ordinary disaster, they'd have stockpiled weapons or enforced a quarantine, but now, anticipating mass insanity, what could they do? Some wept while others quietly resigned themselves to the worst. The city's magistrates ordered tables to be set up in the streets for a final communal feast.

Long after the last pastries had been consumed and while everyone was still lingering there together, an unfamiliar sensa-tion crept over them all with gradually increasing intensity: their thoughts blurred, their bones seemed to fill up with liquid glass, and their limbs ached to lie down.

Of course, reclining was reserved for the Four Prone Activ-ities: undergoing an illness, making love, dying, and giving birth. For these there was one designated pallet on the floor of each home; the rest of the time, everyone was always upright and busy.

"This is it," they lamented. "The fits of insanity will soon be upon us."

Soon they were all lying on the street, motionless as though enchanted. Some time later, they found themselves stirring and sitting up, rubbing their eyes. It felt as though a significant amount of time had passed.

"I was flying low to the ground, and it was hard work but quite ordinary, as though it was something I was used to doing," said one.

"I was about to take a test for a class I'd never attended," said another.

"I looked in the mirror and saw that my teeth had fallen out," said a third.

"All I can remember are incoherent fragments, but I believe at one point I was crossing a border," said yet another.

It was exactly like dreaming, everyone agreed, but looking around, they saw no evidence of frenzy—how was it that there were no broken dishes or overturned chairs, and why was everybody intact without bruises, black eyes, or fractured limbs? Not even their clothing was disarranged!

Though no one knew what to make of the strange collective episode, it was apparently harmless; in fact, they all felt oddly refreshed. Not until it happened again and again, each time after a full cycle of work, play, eating, and cleaning up, did they begin to understand that this was to be a regular occurrence.

While it came as a great relief that there was now no danger of dreamlessness, everyone had to get used to the awkwardness of repeatedly pulling themselves up off the floor with cramped limbs and stiff necks. After a while, the carpenter and the seamstress put their heads together and devised for their families a set of sturdy raised frameworks, each with a supportive rectangular pad for comfort—when word got out, demand immediately exceeded supply, so they had to assign every household a random number to determine the order of distribution.

As people adjusted to the new way of life, they found that this state of suspension could be induced just by lying down, even as it could sometimes be staved off with effort and physical activity so that not everyone was experiencing it at once. That's when gazing at the faces of dreamers became a popular pastime, though no one could understand how it was that this new distance at very close range inspired feelings of intimacy. (A few shy souls chose to don privacy veils when they felt the onset of the heaviness that signaled the change.)

And what should this phenomenon be called? "Dream paralysis," though accurate, seemed unwieldy, but nobody was able to come up with anything better, so they're still debating the matter.

Not all were willing to adapt, however. A few people packed up and left in search of a city still equipped with nets and pulleys. "It's unnatural to separate the life of the body from the life of the soul," they complained, and who are we to gainsay this?

The Remedy for Haunting

You've called in your friends, who entered without a word, tiptoe-ing barefoot one by one through the back door and taking their positions; it requires all your collective subterfuge and speed to successfully rush the ghost, surrounding it as it trembles, blanches, lunges at each of you trying to break through the chain of linked hands, but everyone hangs on tightly while together you chant the digits of pi, since as everyone knows, the presence of irrational numbers causes spectral shrinking and paralysis.

According to federal mandate, of course, you must stop *before* the ghost winks out of existence—plan to fall silent around the five-hundredth digit when your prisoner has dwindled to the size of a standard ice cube, but don't expect the state to take responsibility, even in cases of full-blown infestation.

What to do with all your tiny, freshly immobilized ghosts?

Though some people drive them out to the country, wedging them into the hollows of trees or the crooks of branches, this is generally considered to be inhumane.

Best practice is to suspend them in miniature birdcages throughout your home like a menagerie of pets you never have to feed. Each ghost will emit a stream of inarticulate murmurs and gurgles, a low, continuous burbling sound like that of an old-fashioned office watercooler, not unpleasant despite its doleful resonance, and more effective than the standard white noise machine.

Devices

The inaccessible phone is always just out of reach, caught in a field of mutual repulsion between the desire to communicate and the desire to withhold.

*

Almost too hot to touch, the incandescent phone is powered by rage—there's nothing for it to want and it can't forget anything.

*

This is what every couple needs to maintain rapport: the phone of comprehensive mistranslation.

*

What confessions, recriminations, propositions, ultimatums, and refusals did your device send sizzling into the atmosphere? It's the amnesia phone, so nobody remembers.

*

Like a psychic who channels only Wikipedia, the autodidact phone inserts itself into your conversations to correct, contextualize, disambiguate, a steady chatter audible only to you.

Go into Settings and select a rare, exotic language filter so the phone murmurs in Kawishana or Taushiro, background noise you can almost manage to ignore as though you're strolling through an international airport on your way to your dream destination.

*

Be sure to hit *decline* when the counterfactual phone rings, or all you'll hear about in endless variation is how enviable your life would be if you'd just handled everything differently.

*

Popularly known as the munchkin phone, this unit is so small that you have to manipulate its keyboard with a needle-size stylus in barely discernible movements, an esoteric form of meditation known as pinprick yoga.

*

Used to demonstrate product durability, the widely advertised invincible phone (or, as some call it, the suffering phone) has been repeatedly run over by Nissan Rogue Platinum models, stepped on by obliging elephants, and dropped from prodigious heights. Upon achieving retirement age, it will be released into the maw of an active volcano to melt and congeal with metamorphic cycles; from that point on, it will be known as the molten phone.

*

.

As seen on TV, the mitochondrial phone self-charges by contact with human skin, but what the manufacturers don't disclose is that it efficiently extracts electrical currents from your cell membranes so that the higher the battery level goes, the more depleted you become, until you can't even lift your finger to click on a contact or a link because your body feels heavier than the couch you're unable to peel yourself off of, heavier than the floor beneath the couch, heavier than the foundation of your home, heavier than the earth on which that foundation rests and the 5.5-quintillion-ton atmosphere that surrounds it, heavier than the galaxy, heavier than the universe itself whether it be curved or flat, open or closed, and heavier also than that very question.

*

Ideal for clandestine communication, the transparent phone makes it look like you're talking to yourself.

*

The Casaubon phone holds the key to all mythologies.

*

On the hush phone you speak only with the pre-, post-, and ex-traverbal—that is, infants, the comatose, and those who have tak-en vows of silence. To use it, you press zero-zero-zero, then cover your mouth with your hand as soon as the ringing stops and the whooshing sound lets you know the connection's been made—from then on, you'll proceed solely by mentation.

*

What every ordinary phone fears most is becoming obsolete; soon the entire troposphere will be wired so all you'll have to do to connect with someone is to intone their personal coordinates into the air and then start talking.

But even with direct atmospheric linkage, we'll still count on individual devices for the hybridity of texting in crowded places, like being alone and in company at the same time.

*

A standard prenatal ultrasound scan revealed the amniotic phone budding from a fetus's fingers. Evolutionarily inevitable, it will accompany the child through growth, maturity, senescence, and then into the crematorium (after removal of the battery, which is, of course, highly explosive).

*

Like the legendary Flying Dutchman, the vagrant phone's vocation is to wander on its own itinerary between the absent and the unsought. It never rings twice at the same geographic coordinates.

*

The last-chance phone is what you use while you're describing your city to the barbarians outside the gates: your buildings are decrepit and your roads rife with holes, your water tastes of plastic, and your citizens are too pigeon-toed, bandy-legged, and witless to function as serfs, so clearly, it would be a waste of their time and resources for them to take this city, though of course they'll take it anyway.

*

When you glimpse the insatiable phones flying your way in swarm formation from the edge of visible distance, don't try to run—instead, stand perfectly still. Make your mind as blank as possible, but don't envision anything so nouny as a clean sheet of paper or a cloudless sky; it's absolute emptiness itself you'll need to evoke, since only pure spiritual vacancy will repel them. When you fail at this, they'll attack you with concussive force, battering your skull as they try to breach the bone barrier and gain access to your brain. This kind of phone, from the moment it's hatched, is attracted to information.

*

Everyone pities the liminal phone, doomed to exist painfully on the threshold of sentience without ever crossing over.

*

How refreshing we find it to listen to those medieval midnights that have long since gone extinct in the natural way all nights experience, except those of our current era which are never allowed to ripen and age because we kill them in their infancy with enforced perpetual luminescence, which is why we're driven to aurally connect to that beautiful, unwired obscurity accessible only through the Dark Ages phone.

*

The Zen phone arrives encased in a waxy rind you have to slice with your fingernail, or if that's not sharp enough, with a blade, and then you dig in to peel it away chunk by chunk despite its resistance—you're sweating by the time you've gotten it all off, but look, there's another coating beneath it, mottled, nubbly, and even more difficult to penetrate, and your determination knows no bounds though your fingers are starting to cramp. Beneath that layer is the silk rind which, despite its delicacy and sheerness, proves to be the most adhesive of all. Paradoxically, you could whisper-nudge it off only with the very lightest of touches, but you always refrain, too shy to glimpse what's underneath: your phone's Original Face.

*

Though everyone knows that the mere presence of a cell phone significantly reduces cognitive function, no one's willing to live without one or even power it down and shut it away in a drawer for an hour. Desperate to protect the intelligence still remaining in the world, all the tech companies have joined forces to create the quantum phone, synched with your brain waves so that it pops into existence only when someone calls you or when you want to use it—after that, it pops right back out.

Upon purchasing this device, you have to preselect the level of intent that will summon it. Some people set it at one for the mildest of mental itches, a few noble souls choose eleven for the desperation of a life-threatening emergency, but most pick a number somewhere between those extremes. Where the phone lives the rest of the time is anybody's guess.

*

The negation phone is every phone that wasn't invented in time to convey apologies, declarations of passion, blood-test results, massive shifts in the macroeconomic outlook, pertinent information about latitude, longitude, and elevation, and all the other nominal, ordinal, discreet, and continuous data on whose absence we can blame battles lost, patients succumbed, lovers not reunited. We grip the shape of its absence as we weep.

*

But who doesn't long for the lupine phone, on which you hear the distant howling of your pack?

*

Keepers

If no one had invented the personal alarm device, you'd have to hire a human timekeeper.

Depending on your deadline's proximity, your keeper might have enough margin to stroll away from you, get a haircut, work out at the gym, and pick up a few groceries, all the while calculating the distance between the two of you against the remaining seconds, or maybe they'd stick close, dogging your footsteps, grabbing the adjacent table at Starbucks, following you home to lean against the bathroom door while you floss your teeth.

Though timekeeping would be considered an honorable profession, the burnout rate would be so high that perhaps we should imagine this work as reciprocal instead—you'd keep time for me one day, I'd keep time for you the next, a connection more intense than even the most enmeshed love affair.

The seeds for this arrangement would be sown as adolescents first start to become responsible for their schedules, awkwardly drifting together in shy experimental pairings, practice runs for the lifelong commitment formalized at the age of majority. During this period, each teen would try out various ways of announcing "time's up" to their partner: mime style with dramatic gesticulations culminating in a full-body bow, for instance, or musically, playing a brief and sprightly passage on their pocket ocarina, or by the classic three-tap pattern on the left shoulder blade . . . Later in life, of course, this work would become increasingly subtle; even if you could gaze unblinkingly for weeks at a pair of aged time-mates, you wouldn't be able to observe the announcement since it would be so intricately woven into the pattern of their shared interactions that it could be recognized only from within the relationship—a particular kind of sigh, a slight shift in vocal tone, a slow and singular glance.

Despite the theoretically inviolable nature of the adult dyad, however, every now and then a particular pairing might fray or even snap. Appointments would be missed; library books would accrue exorbitant overdue fines; sleep and meal patterns would become erratic; the skin would grow patchy, the eyes dim, the molars loose. In such cases, only the most rigidly conservative citizens would even think of denying these sufferers a swift temporal divorce in order to seek more compatible partners.

Even more rare would be those individuals born with their own internal clockwork, a measurement-sense so finely calibrated that they'd be able to stand alone. Though a few people would be jealous—oh, the insouciance, the independence!—most would pity them. "How flat, how flavorless their lives must be," some neighbors would whisper, and "How selfish!" others would murmur, despite treating them with elaborate courtesy since that's what civilized persons do, all the while wondering whether the mavericks are actually human: it's unnatural to survive on a steady diet of time without intimacy.

The Self-Correcting Language

Almost everyone was happy when the bioengineers released it into the population, even editors and grammarians whose jobs were rendered obsolete, their purehearted love of accuracy transcending their own self-interest. It's true that a few alarmists were concerned about the way it consumed all other languages as it crackled through the population's synapses, but against such ferocity and speed, what recourse could there be?

Now words are never misspelled, sentences don't get knotted and gnarled, and the backspace and delete keys are no longer included on the newest keyboards, just as Microsoft Word Track Changes and Google Docs have been relegated to the Archives of Computer History, and everyone remembers them with the same condescension previous generations felt toward AOL.

Of course, it's still possible to lie, but only with exquisite clarity, pristine syntax, and formidable structure, not a word or inflection out of place, all nuances of implication in exquisite harmony. The most mundane conversation is like that folktale in which diamonds, pearls, and roses fall from between the heroine's lips when she speaks.

And as though to live up to this aesthetic upgrade, people have quit throwing soda cans from their car windows and dropping cigarette butts and fast-food wrappers in parking lots. Even the most egregious absentee landlords have shamefacedly arranged for repairs, fresh paint, and landscaping. New buildings are sleeker and brighter, and for the most part, citizens treat each other more honorably, inspired by the nobility of their shared speech.

So why is the underground movement in favor of a contraband coarse and fallible language gaining such momentum? (It's been rumored that foreign agitators have infiltrated the populace to stir things up, a titillating possibility indeed, but looking around, everyone sees only the same familiar faces.) The truth is that now that the novelty has worn off, people are dissatisfied with the mouthfeel of this angelically refreshing speech, so light, so silky smooth, delicate as the finest sherbet. An innate chthonic tendency has reasserted itself in favor of a lumpy, gritty language apparently seasoned with flakes of coal, flecks of clay, and fragments of crushed glass; the soul craves the texture of trouble on the tongue.

The Sky Is Lifting

When people first noticed the sky tearing loose from the ground, everyone rose to the occasion; wherever you looked, you could see teams of workers staggering under granite slabs, piling up the pyramids to tamp it down at the ripped places.

Thousands of years later when another cluster of small unseamings appeared, the great cathedrals of Europe were plunked down over them, those bulky limestone arpeggios with their buttresses, rose windows, gargoyles, and grotesques.

But by the time yet this most recent wound appeared, life had become so universally complex and demanding that the only people who noticed were those residing in its vicinity—for a while, they simply kept an eye on the damage, but one day, someone inserted the tip of a pair of tweezers into the torn place and then pulled it back out again covered with a cobwebby substance none of them could identify, more gummy than fluid. Somebody even put a lit match to the stuff, but it wouldn't burn, only bubbled and smoked a little, which, everyone said, was just as well, since the last thing they needed was for some idiot to set all of heaven aflame in its sheathing like old attic insulation. Meanwhile, the tear was starting to branch and spread, allowing the sticky substance to ooze out around the edges.

Nobody liked the idea of having only the fraying sky between them and whatever might be burgeoning on the other side, so they decided to try to hold down the firmament. Lacking recourse to deposits of granite and limestone, they sought the heaviest objects locally available, both of which were housed in the region's main attraction, the Museum of Musical Anomalies: the world's largest piano ("tensile stress of strings thirty tons, weight one ton") and the world's heaviest marimba, made entirely of superdense crystal, and possessing a range of eleven octaves. These were painstakingly disassembled, conveyed in parts, reassembled, and set down along the Lines of Severance. To make the town's children feel included in the project, the mayor arranged for a long chain of kindergarteners to pull a red wagon carrying the world's smallest autoharp, originally built for a royal family's dollhouse. Constructed from balsa wood scraps and plated with gold hammered almost to the point of transparency, it was tinier than a matchbox, so light that the curators had to place it in a miniature tent to protect it from breezes.

But public distress hit an all-time high when the presence of these heavy items failed to heal the rift. Was there no hope, no recourse? However, though most of the people assumed that the sky was simply refusing to accept the substitution of the one-ton piano, etc., for the standard pyramid or cathedral, those few who had committed themselves to actually measure and log the crack's growth patterns announced that it was slowing down in the vicinity of the autoharp!

After extensive debate, the group concluded that the sky had experienced so many internal transformations throughout its history that the treatments used in long-ago millennia would be inappropriate to its present nature—what to do with a sky of such exquisite sensibilities, a sky which apparently preferred string to percussion?—clearly, it had to be humored, even pampered, so they again raided the museum, this time for the famed Monster Cello of Dublin and the world's largest playable guitar, a Gibson Flying V which they also placed atop the crack, but alas, their effort was in vain.

It must be, they said, that the sky fancies not the autoharp's strings but its molecular composition; they melted several vaults' worth of bullion bars and bricks, as well as assorted brooches, earrings, bracelets, pendants, coins, medals, trophies, retirement watches, and tiny heirloom Christmas-tree angels into an enormous, dense, and singularly unattractive glob of lumpen gold, which they placed on the growing edge of the crack to no avail.

The people were stumped as the crack's growth began to accelerate. Yes, they were all doomed. Tragically, no one understood that what had proven to be so medicinal about the autoharp was simply the fact that it was so insubstantial, nearly weightless. Though the sky could no longer respond to anything dense or ponderous, the tear would have begun to seal over if anyone had simply brushed it with the whisper-light tip of a feather from a hummingbird's wing.

Hatchling

The larval flute is exhausted from straining to sprout holes. Though it understands that every musical instrument in the whole world had to undergo a similar process, it can't help but wonder— is there a holding place somewhere for lopsided violins and violas, gap-toothed pianos, clapperless handbells, unhollow drums?

Is the larval flute destined to join them, and if so, what kind of ailing music could they make together? Everything, no matter how raw or ill formed, is required to sing.

Product Details

This is a softcover volume of paperboard construct. There may be bucklings or stains on the binding or spine. Page corners may be creased from prior use. The cover may be slightly bent or frayed. The book may display tattoos, piercings, abrasions, lacerations, flash burns, and signs of gangrene or necrosis. You may note tooth marks of beasts, toddlers, and bibliovampires interrupted mid-devotion. There may be marginalia—memoranda, confessions, manifestos, and teardrop residue, either subtle individual puckers or rivulets from copious weeping (don't attempt to scrape off any mosses and lichens; these can provide augmented oxygenation as you read). We may have inadvertently neglected to extract pharmaceuticals, prophylactics, strands of human hair, infant socks, silk eye masks, star maps, bathymetric graphs, and the crinkly translucent wrappers of gourmet candy. We don't provide a volume's pedigree or medical history, nor do we disclose the location of its psyche, which may stretch like an invisible membrane along the hinge, or parcel itself out in punctuation, or glint off the white space as subsurface scattering.

Upon arrival, your book will be weary and agitated, in need of succor. Switch off your HVAC—text just out of transit can't endure temperature change, the sensation of air moving across its surfaces, or any other episode analogous to weather. Prepare a nest of gently warmed towels never exposed to bleach or fabric softeners, then swathe your newcomer in darkness and compressed biological silence while it steeps in a fantasy of oblivion, allowing twenty-four hours of dormancy per page, not excluding front matter and indices.

Deprived of this treatment, a book may quiver and wail; it may babble, divulging spoilers; it may regress to experience the phantom pains and pleasures of trees, and so somnambulate, attempt incremental migration, creeping across the coffee table as forests traverse continents. Or, panicking, it may spring a significance-leak that can't be plugged no matter how many transfusions you try from volumes you've deemed expendable. In such cases, we never accept returns, since due to the rise of reader callousness and impulsivity, we'd be overwhelmed with the sufferings of mishandled books. We're a clearinghouse, not a hospice!

But where, we ask, are the readers of yesteryear eager to give each book its full recovery time, planning each purchase according to the hibernation schedule of their wish-list titles? Where is what used to be known as *the gentle reader*?

In a just universe, books would have evolved to shed their sensitivity, their craving for seclusion; by now each one would have learned to cop an attitude, daring any abusive or neglectful owner to crack it open so it could leap up to beat against the face with its covers, the page corners going for the eyes.

Hurt

How surprising so late in history to discover a new kind of pain!

It's not limited to a particular limb or organ, and it doesn't match anything in the standard taxonomy: burning, stabbing, aching, pulsating, stinging, cramping . . .

Instead, it's a sense of compression that torments us when we're doing only one thing at a time instead of concurrently watching a movie, cooking, eating, responding to texts, emails, and phone calls, editing our digital images, balancing our accounts, vacuuming, updating our calendars, toggling between online games.

Tragically, there's no therapeutic protocol. No emergency room, pain-management clinic, or insurance company will touch it. The only thing a sufferer can do is to revert to multitasking, which instantly releases head-to-toe surges of somatic relief.

But nobody knows how to feel about those rare ascetics who voluntarily limit their activities for extended intervals.

Take, for instance, Maximillian of reality-show fame, who endured forty days and forty nights of doing no more than two things at once!

We all kept the feed on in the background throughout his ordeal, glancing over at it now and then just as we'd done during the ground war; the gestation, birth, and infancy of the pandas in the zoo; the rescue team's eleven-day underground endeavor to find the film star who'd fallen through a mine shaft; and the gloriously titillating Esperanto Society sex scandal. But whenever Maximillian signaled that he would temporarily limit himself to *just one activity or device* for a few minutes, we'd drop everything to gather around our screens, gasping and clutching each other as the experience of watching him suffer became so intense we had to turn away.

Each day the collective pain threshold drops as our bodies demand an ever-increasing number of simultaneous activities to maintain equilibrium.

Though this is quite a challenge for some of us, our children move so swiftly that they often seem to blur before our very eyes! Day and night, we race to catch up to them, clocking each other with unflagging zeal, administering neighborly motivational punishments when anyone slackens—we must all transition together to the high-velocity dimension that's just beyond our current level of awareness.

Then the Maximillians of this world will look around to find themselves alone amid the throng of our devices, their fixed and stalwart family.

Bread

According to the owner of the tiny but legendary Esoteric Bake-shop, men created the early breads to be solid, compact, but when villages first began to war against each other, the women who took over the work of food production proved more inventive than their mates, bestowing an inner life on their handiwork—thus, almost as soon as there was bread there were pockets in bread for charms, runes, amulets, beads, miniature carved gods, tiny lethal blades, medicinal and toxic herbs, and then, much later, maps, codes, diamonds, keys, cash, cigarettes, tiny bottles of bootleg liquor, the finest cocaine . . .

What the Esoteric Baker slips into each loaf is a story inscribed with edible ink on rice paper in her clear, narrow script. Where the stories come from, she won't say—the only bit of information she's divulged (even to the *New York Times* feature writer) is that she never repeats a tale. And every day, the line of eager customers winds around three city blocks.

This is how it works. All the way home from her shop, you cradle your first loaf, a humble baguette fresh from the oven, silky, pliant, and aromatic as an infant—adding even butter would be a travesty! The instant you have it alone in your kitchen, you rip it apart to excavate and open the scroll, gorging yourself on delectable bread-flesh while you read in a rush what you recognize as the story for which you've been waiting your whole life without even knowing; it refreshes; it enlivens, and though tears of delight season the bread, you're too engrossed to even wipe your eyes.

And then it's over. For a moment, you stand there sighing and savoring the tonal aftertaste. You long to read it again, or at least pull out your cell phone and take a photo, but faithful to the bizarre purchasing agreement, you roll up the parchment and pop it into your mouth. Swift to dissolve, it slides fluidly down your throat, and then all at once, dialogue, characters, imagery, and plot disappear from your memory. What was it that you just read, what was it that moved you so? Like everyone else, of course, you've heard that the Esoteric Baker designs her narratives to turn mentally invisible upon consumption; you'd assumed that was just a combination of advertising hype and urban mythology, but now all that remains is the sensation of having been immersed in a tale of unparalleled wonder without even a trace of its content.

But the story itself is ecstatic! This is narrative apotheosis—to be housed, yet free from the onerous human gaze! As you resolve to save up for another loaf, it begins to expand in your darkness.

Tribe

From early childhood on, we've proven less than proficient at games requiring hair-trigger reflexes, physical agility, and accurate recall of numbers, patterns, or sequences; at activities requiring large or small motor coordination, static or dynamic balance, rhythm, muscular fortitude, speed, propulsion of objects, self, or others, and calculating multiple moves ahead; bidding, bluffing, miming, sliding, guarding, pitching, catching, chanting, dimensional perception and projection, manipulation of the laws of probability, and conversance with popular culture.

We excel in activities requiring lassitude, distractibility, clapping off the beat, vertigo, misspeaking, self-igniting, narcolepsy, a viscous roiling amnesia, the inability to refrain from simultaneously generating and falling into apertures of indeterminate sizes and configurations while dowsing for sky in the sky, and the knack of getting the punch line long after everyone else has gone home.

Yes, laughing alone in an empty room: any of us might enthusiastically compete at that.

Anomalous Teeth

One day each year, a floating day that nobody can predict, everyone wakes up with an alien set of teeth perfectly fitted to their own gums as though they'd been there all along.

A woman smiles at her morning coffee date, revealing the shiny black tines of an Ace comb.

Posed in front of an illuminated projection of swirls and arrows, a weather forecaster parts his lips to prognosticate, displaying a row of steel ingots.

A baby's open-mouthed chortle exposes a shrunken version of her grandmother's dentures while the grandmother sports just two tiny painful buds.

In the bathroom mirror, a teenager finds himself elated to discover that his spiky orthodontured array has been replaced by sharks' blades, incurved and double layered.

Throughout the day, behavior is so unpredictable that a spirit of universal forbearance prevails; contracts drawn up and marriages entered into can be dissolved without consequence the next morning when everyone awakens to the sensation of their own ordinary teeth.

For most, this is as euphoric as being reunited with a beloved after a prolonged and agonizing search, which is why that day instantly turns into a festival. Songs and speeches collide uproariously in the air, and long dessert tables crowd the streets.

But every year, at least one citizen realizes they'd have preferred to retain the previous day's changes despite their own bizarre appearance and the difficulties with speaking and eating. Sadly, however, this isn't possible; the visitant teeth were always only just passing through.

Immersion Candles

They illuminate inverse baptisms, subaqueous weddings and funerals, a custodian sweeping the ocean floor, a woman unbraiding her hair at a salt mirror, children tumbling together in fish-gold grottos.

Brightest underwater, they must be routinely lifted into the air lest they too swiftly consume themselves. The candle-bearers who work in staggered rotations to raise and lower them are those natural loners who before the Great Descent would have been night watchmen, lighthouse keepers, cattle herders. Though they retain no collective memories of life before the whole human race migrated down the stairs of the sea, that ancient professional silence protocol remains; passing one another among bioluminescent jellyfish in the mesopelagic zone, they merely nod without making eye contact and keep moving.

The New Self-Soothing

The earth was able to breathe again when we'd finished feeding the sky our cobweb-cracked smartphones, chipped CorningWare, scalped Barbies and American Girls, the smidgens and scraps of our inconvenient, incriminating, and obsolete information, and the very last crumbs of toxic waste. Without subtle veiling from the off-gasses emitted from millennia of clutter, everything seemed paradoxically roomier and more intimate than before, people's faces so vivid that we found ourselves shaken. No wonder we had accumulated the artifactual overflow of history itself, craving its atmospheric haze as a buffer between us. The unmitigated human presence—who could bear it? That's when we began to avert our eyes from each other and shrink away.

Now we comfort ourselves by standing shouting distance apart as we gaze through our individual handheld monocular telescopes at the junk stream above us, calling out when we glimpse a familiar configuration: "Look, aren't those Great-Aunt Ellen's VHS Christmas tapes?" "Of course—it's the end of April, just when they always pass by!"

But once or twice in a generation, meteorologists send out warnings about a discontinuity in the trash currents, a traveling gap of naked sky. Many of the people in its path run indoors and yank down their shades to shield themselves from the traumatic sight. (For those who miss the alert and happen to catch a glimpse of sheer pellucid blue, of clouds, of night with its uncanny distant lights, there are treatment centers from which few return.) Others stand on their lawns blindfolded, faces lifted—a few chant arcane verses from *The Dread and Worshipful Book of the Firmament*, but everyone else aims their long-range precision rifles at the depthless vacancy passing overhead.

The End of Shopping

After the end of shopping, a lot of people left town, though if you'd stopped them to ask why, they wouldn't have been able to name anything they needed since the Committee in Charge distributes all goods fairly; their decisions are regulated and enforced by a rotating cadre of ninja ethicists who had to be hunted down and driven out of the obscure places where they were hiding in hopes of not having to monitor anyone or (especially) attend any meetings.

So why did these neighbors abscond in their RVs? They were convinced that there must be someplace in this great nation where shopping is still possible, though it's not the actual items they crave but the sensation of exchange for consumer goods since without that, they don't feel human. According to rumor, they've joined up with seekers from other towns to form a great caravan snaking back and forth across the country in search of the legendary Phantom Mall, which supposedly materializes out of nothing on random nights, sometimes years apart, complete with kiosks, fountains, food courts, and piped-in ambient music, lingering for a while only to unpredictably vanish along with everyone in it, a risk the perpetual caravanners are willing to take. Of course, we can't help but wonder about the condition of the mall's patrons while it's in its unmanifest state—do they continue to physically age, insensate, soft pretzels and designer tote bags in hand, triply reflected before Neiman Marcus dressing room mirrors so that they have trouble recognizing themselves when they awaken as the mall reappears hundreds of miles from where it was last sighted?

As for those of us who've stayed put, we spend our time making lavish gourmet desserts for the ninja ethicists to compensate them for their conscription and creating a more salutary version of the shopping experience because it's innate in our species to stroll through a commodious public space perusing an array of assorted items and glancing curiously, though surreptitiously, at other faces. That's why every Saturday we line the streets with long tables laden with arts and crafts, breads, cakes, pies, and household goods we no longer want but which other people might find amusing, beautiful, or useful. After we've allotted ourselves a limited number of colorful handmade vouchers with arbitrary values, we wander around picking things up, examining them, and putting them down in favor of other things, a few of which we place in baskets to take home for the week. Then we adjourn to our community hub, the stripped-down Big Lots distribution center, for a potluck meal.

Some of our elders still remember the Great Labor of rooting out from among us all evidence of the bad old days of planned obsolescence and conspicuous consumption—the video footage, the digital data, the glossy magazines now stored in the Forbidden Library in a secret subbasement of the county courthouse. We're careful to present to our children a fabricated history in which things have always been as they are now; in fact, to refer to the former existence of capitalism or mention any of its components within hearing range of an underage citizen is punishable by execution, not in public but secretly by poison so that to all appearances, the death is caused by a stroke or heart attack, though the adults know the real story. Though we don't *enjoy* reporting on each other's lapses any more than we relish our regularly scheduled turns on the neighborhood watch's assassination rotation (everyone longs for an uneventful year of duty!), we understand how crucial it is to safeguard the young ones' ethical faculties. (Don't think for even a moment that we don't miss our neighbors—most recently, Frances "Biddie" Farmer, Henderson Doyle Herrick, Jr., known simply as "H.," Toni Rae Blakely, and others—overheard inadvertently letting indiscretions slip within earshot of the young.)

When a group of children comes of age, they're awakened in the night, blindfolded, and taken to the Forbidden Library to learn about how compound interest, double-cycle billing, and EMV chips nearly destroyed the natural world; they're shown clips of overflowing landfills, dried-up riverbeds, and the sky as it used to be, so cluttered with delivery drones that the very idea of constellations almost went extinct along with the eagles and the wolves. One by one, they tremblingly swear to preserve our way of life by regularly taking their place on the watch. And each new batch of initiates (often in tears, always with tremulous bewilderment) asks the same question, the only one we can't answer: "But all that 'money'—was it even real?"

Telling

In their bed in the darkened room, the lovers hold themselves scarcely a breath apart; skin-to-skin contact would be overwhelming as they summon up their nerve to break the secrecy taboo. In this land where women experience the passage of time in tangible ways, it's unthinkable to disclose these perceptions to any male, which is why her voice trembles as she whispers: "On some days, time is particulate matter falling like blue snow that makes the air smell of ozone."

Listening, he knows that anything he could say would shatter the moment of forbidden intimacy, so he holds his breath to keep himself from asking what it's like to behold time flurrying around her indoors and out. It's no wonder she frequently seems . . . not aloof, exactly, but abstracted, slightly removed, as though enclosed by a private silence. His fists clench with the urgency of his desire to join her inside that blue veil—but then almost immediately he envisions himself grabbing her by the hand and pulling, pulling, with all his strength, wrenching her out of it towards himself; shame at this image of violation suffuses him as he struggles to subdue his emotions lest she somehow intuit them.

Now she's whispering again. "On other days, time is a wolf pack. No matter what I'm doing—brewing my coffee, filing a report—at the edge of my consciousness, I sense them loping to-gether across the tundra; I hear their great hearts beating."

Yes, he thinks, that explains it. He's often been aware of some unreachable otherness within her, but now that he knows her se-cret, surely with patience and strategy, he can gain access to that part of her, tame and subdue it . . . He recoils from the thought, then wonders uneasily—with these impulses in himself to sup-press, to hide, how can their union endure?

"But usually," she says, "time is a tiny glass needle so heavy that it takes all my strength to lift it as I puncture the air again and again to make stitches of invisible thread, but I'm not allowed to stop. All through my workday and even while I sleep, that's what I'm really doing inside."

Bitterly, he castigates himself for casually disregarding her sub-terranean layers of exhaustion. Oh, if only he could trade places with her! For him, time has always been a straight, forward-moving line, occasionally speeding up or slowing down a bit, but mostly proceeding at a steady rate—how comparatively restful she would find this!

"It used to be," she tells him as though having read his mind, "that men and women knew time together; it was the end of this arrangement that marked the beginning of history. It's said that women stole these sensations from men because they felt the need to relieve men of the burden, restoring their innocence, or that men found the experience so disorienting that they gave it up . . . The stories go on and on! There are exactly one hundred of them, and the year each girl comes of age, she has to memorize them all."

Awed that she carries so many versions of their people's past within her, he wonders: has he known her only superficially, and his previous lovers, and his mother and his sisters as well? He thinks of his parents' marriage, all those decades together of one-sided ignorance. In the darkness, he covers his face with his hands. If only he could go back to the moment just before she'd told him, he'd be secure again, happy in their love, but it would be an illusion.

Nevertheless, would he? ... Would he?

Epochal

Pulling out of the driveway in their Dodge Durango, my neighbors are all set for a Civil War reenactment, the dad and sons in Confederate grays, the mom and daughters in hoop skirts and bonnets.

If this were the nineteenth century, though, they'd be dressing up as Redcoats, Continental soldiers or maybe even Hessian mercenaries. In the 1700s, it was all the rage to don Renaissance-style ruffs, codpieces, feathers, and voluminous skirts, while during the Renaissance itself, they romanticized the Middle Ages, donning coifs and tunics and as much plate armor as they could bear.

Back and back and back it goes, but time is circular, not linear, which is why the Neanderthals painted cave walls with images of humanoid figures in astronaut helmets, memorializing their nostalgia for the future.

Fathoming

In one sequence, Orpheus follows Eurydice into the underworld to retrieve her; in another, Orpheus has died and Eurydice goes in after him equipped not with a lyre, but with a basket full of honey cakes and a cut-glass flask of ouzo to beguile Hades.

And so, the lovers trade places in version after version, each of them true, all of them overlapping until they've passed themselves coming and going in ghost light so many times that suddenly, they decide they've had enough, so they fuse into a single pair.

Now instead of venturing upward yet again, they turn to descend even deeper, leaving Hades gape jawed above them on his obsidian throne agleam in infernal light.

They clamber bloody handed down subterranean frozen waterfalls.

They sidestroke through the thirty-one shades of black in abysmal rivers, almost parting ways over which is more luscious, onyx or ebony.

They feel their way through labyrinthine grottoes, feeding each other the delicate flesh of what will centuries later be called *bébés champignons de l'oubli*—pale, flavorful morels that cause them to suffer through the seven stages of forgetfulness and then back into memories which may or may not be the same.

They stagger like sleepwalkers through the molten core, beholding each other limned in flame.

They suffer vertigo when *down* becomes *up* as they struggle toward the surface on the opposite side, arguing over what this might mean about the shape of the world.

They endure the most harrowing passage of all, a monotonous granite road that seems to slope on forever.

At last, they push themselves out through a karst into open air to stand aching, upright.

Soon they'll look around, even dare to reacquaint themselves with the sky, but for now they gaze only at each other in the natural morning light that stings their eyes, familiar and strange as any couple.

One Sleep

Four Poster Bed, by Andrew Wyeth (USA) 1946

He painted beds without sleepers and sleepers without beds, the recumbent and reclining, his subjects laid out, tipped back, on swings, in boats, in melting snowdrifts, in grass and leaves and soil, the flourishing and dying, the trapped and tranced.

Of his early years, he said, *I was sick in bed so much of my life . . . I'd feel the stretch of the bedclothes over the mattress. And pillows always seemed like big mountains to me*—interiority as land-scape, convalescence as connective tissue in the body of time.

Be sure you look at me in death, his father told him, yet he painted the sleeping Helga nude in his father's coffin, a kind of hypnagogic transposition he hid for over a decade.

I think there's more chance of getting motion by stillness than by a thing that has great speed, he said, and decades later, of his mother-in-law's passing: *I felt the whole bed would drift out that front door and down to the river . . .*

But while this strange half bed stays rooted, does the room approach or recede? Here is the house of dream: simultaneous exposure and concealment; scumble of shadows in suspension; spans of glass and chenille rendered reticent, austere; that astrin-gent northern light a form of indirect address—how many veils of transparency does visible silence require?

Against washes of distressed plaster, sightlines trouble the eye as everything tilts downward to the right, though we would not wish it all fresh, adorned, well lit. The sojourner at the threshold needs this stripped-down space, the enigma of missing knobs and latches, the accumulated sleep of the other always opening deeper in.

Acknowledgments

The following have been published, some in previous iterations in:

"The Pillow Museum" and "Devices," *New Ohio Review*

"Tune-up" and "Home Art," Ruler's Wit *Dark and Light* Anthology

"Elemental," *Third Wednesday*

"Monograph for a Giant Lullaby," *Dark Mountain*

"Dig," *MacQueens Quinterly*

"Gravity Pajamas," *Bacopa Literary Review*

"The Fleet Ones," "Universal Cognitive Maintenance," "Pockets," and "Relics," *The Fabulist*

"Shore Patrol" and "Immersion Candles," *Redheaded Stepchild*

"Keepers," *Laurel Review*

"Passage," *Lucky 7: The Ekphrastic Marathon Anthology*

"Going Under," *Glacier*

"Donations" and "A Remedy for Haunting," *Prose Poems*

"A Day's Work," "Crossings," and "Forests," *Cherry Tree: A National Literary Journal @ Washington College*, Issue 9, 2023

"One Sleep," *The Ekphrastic Review*

"Recurrence," "Fathoming," and "Literary Contrivances of the Future," *The Mackinaw*

"Relics," *The Fabulist Flash* and *The Fabulist Book of Miniatures, vol. 1*

"Quotations attributed to Andrew Wyeth in the story "One Sleep" from Andrew Wyeth: A Secret Life by Richard Meryman (HarperCollins, 1996).

Thanks for editorial suggestions and/or inspiration from Gil Allen, Jon Bateman, Sarah Blackman, Dorothy Beling, Diana Goetsch, Mark Halliday, Lorette C. Luzajic, Cathy Parrill, Jim Peterson, Meg Pokrass, Susan Tekulve, Dave Wanczyk, and Josh Wilson.